P9-DDC-875

# Our Twisted Hero

# Our Twisted Hero

*Yi Munyol*

TRANSLATED BY KEVIN O'ROURKE

Printed in the United States of America. For information address Hyperion, 77 W. 66th Street, New York, New York 10023-6298.

Library of Congress Cataloging-in-Publication Data

Yi, Munyol
[Uridul ui ilgurojin yongung. English]
Our twisted hero / Yi Munyol ; translated by Kevin O'Rourke.—1st ed.
p. cm.
ISBN 0-7868-6670-5
1. Totalitarianism—Fiction. I. O'Rourke, Kevin. II. Title.
PL992.9.M83 O8713 2001
895.7'34—dc21 00-044848

FIRST EDITION

Designed by Debbie Glasserman

10 9 8 7 6 5 4 3 2 1

# Our Twisted Hero

IT'S BEEN NEARLY THIRTY YEARS ALREADY, but whenever I look back on that lonely, difficult fight, which continued from the spring of that year through the fall, I become as desolate and gloomy as I was at the time. Somehow in our lives we seem to get into fights like this all the time, and perhaps I get this feeling because to this day I've never really extricated myself from *that* one.

Around the middle of March that year, when the Liberal Party government was making its last stand, I left the prestigious Seoul elementary school I had proudly attended until then and transferred to a rather undistinguished school in a small town. My whole family had moved there after my father, a civil servant, had become embroiled in an internal departmental row. I was twelve; I had just gone into fifth grade.

When I arrived there that first day, escorted by my mother, I was enormously disappointed, for all sorts of reasons, by S Elementary School. I was used to looking at new school buildings arranged around an imposing three-story red-brick main building. To me, this old Japanese-style building, with its plastered exterior and its few ramshackle tar-painted board classrooms, seemed indescribably shabby. It drenched me in a kind of melodramatic disillusion a young prince lately deposed might feel. The mere fact that I came from a school where each grade had sixteen classes made me look with disdain on this school where there were barely six classes in a grade. Also, having studied in classes of boys and girls mixed together, to find boys' classes and girls' classes strictly segregated seemed very backward.

But it was the faculty room that really hardened my first impression. The faculty room of the school I had attended, as befitted one of the top schools in Seoul, was big and sparkling, and the teachers were all uniformly well-groomed and full of life. Here, the faculty room was barely the size of a classroom and the teachers in it sat lifelessly, shabby country folk blowing out smoke like chimneys.

As soon as my mother brought me into the room, the teacher in charge came over to greet us. He too fell far short of my expectations. If we couldn't have a beautiful and kind female teacher, I thought at least we might have a soft-spoken, considerate, stylish male one. But the white rice-wine stain on the sleeve of his jacket told me he didn't measure up. His hair was tousled; he had not combed it much less put oil on it. It was very doubtful if he had washed his face that morning, and his physical attitude left grave doubts about whether he was actually listening to Mother. Frankly, it was indescribably disappointing that such a man was to be my new teacher. Perhaps already I had a premonition of the evil that was to unfold over the course of the next year.

That evil showed itself days later when I was being introduced to the class.

"This is the new transfer student, Han Pyongt'ae. I hope you get on well."

The teacher, having concluded this one line introduction, seated me in an empty chair in the back and went directly into classwork. When I thought of how considerate my Seoul teachers had been in invariably giving prolonged proud introductions to new students, almost to the point of embarrassment, I could not hold back my disappointment. He didn't have to give me a big buildup, but he could at least have told the other children about some of the things I had to my credit. It would have helped me begin to relate to the others and them to me.

There were a couple of things the teacher could have mentioned. First of all, there was my schoolwork. I may not have been first very often, but I was in the first five in my class in an outstanding Seoul school. I was quietly proud of this; it had played no small part in ensuring good results in my relations not only with teachers but also with the other children. I was also very good at painting. I was not good enough to sweep a national children's art contest, but I did get the top award in a number of contests at the Seoul level. I presume my mother stressed my marks and artistic ability several times, but the teacher ignored them completely. In some circumstances, my father's job, too, could have been a help. So what if he had suffered a setback in Seoul, even a bad one, bad enough to drive him from Seoul to here? He still ranked with the top few civil servants in this small town.

Disappointingly, the boys were just like the teacher. In Seoul when a new transfer student arrived, the other children took advantage of the first break in class to surround him and ask all sorts of questions: Are you good at school? Are you strong? Are you well off? They asked questions like these to gather the basic materials for establishing a relationship later on. But my new classmates, like my new teacher, had little interest in this. At the break they stood at a distance stealing quick glances across. And when finally at lunchtime a few boys did gather around, it was only to ask whether I had been on a tram, had seen South Gate, and other questions of this sort. In fact, the only things they seemed envious of, or impressed by, were my school supplies. These were of high quality and I was the only one who had them.

But to this day, nearly thirty years later, what makes the memory of that first day so vivid in my mind was my meeting with Om Sokdae.

"Get out of the way, all of you!"

The few children were ringed around me in the classroom asking their questions when suddenly a low voice sounded softly from behind them. It was a grown-up voice, sufficiently so for me to wonder if the teacher had come back. The children flinched and stepped back abruptly. I was taken by surprise, too. I turned around in my chair and saw a boy sitting at a desk at the back of the middle row; he was solidly planked down there and he looked at us with a certain air of resignation.

We had only been in class together for an hour, but I knew this fellow. From the way he shouted "Attention! Salute!" when the teacher came in, I presumed he was the class monitor. The other reason I could distinguish him immediately among the nearly sixty students in the class, all of whom were much the same size, was that sitting down he seemed a head taller than any of the other boys—and his eyes seemed to burn into me.

"Han Pyongt'ae, you said, right? Come here."

He spoke once again in that same soft but firm voice. That was all; he didn't move a finger; and yet

I found myself almost getting up. Such was the strange effect his eyes had on me.

I braced myself, with the shrewd sophistication of a Seoulite. My first fight, I thought, and with this sudden realization came a determination to see it through to the end. If I let myself be seen as easy prey from the beginning, I figured life here would be difficult. But could I fight back in the face of the baffling, virtually absolute obedience of the others?

"What do you want?" I answered defiantly, pulling in my tummy; he just snickered contemptuously.

"I want to ask you something," he said.

"If you want to ask something, come on over here then."

"What?"

The corners of his eyes suddenly arched as if to say that he'd heard everything now; again he snickered. He said no more; he just looked at me quietly, his eyes glued to me so intensely that it was difficult to meet them. But I had come too far to back down now. This too is a kind of fight, I thought, bracing myself with all my strength. Two of the bigger boys who were sitting beside him got up and came over to me.

"Get up!"

They both looked angry. It seemed as if they might pounce on me at any moment. Any way I looked at it, I wouldn't be able to take on both of them. Suddenly I was on my feet. One of them grabbed me roughly by the collar and shouted, "Didn't Om Sokdae, the class monitor, tell you to come over?"

This was the first time I had heard the name Om Sokdae. It was engraved on my memory from the moment I heard it, perhaps because of the odd tone of voice the boy used to pronounce it. It was as if he were using the name of someone very great and noble, as if respect and obedience for such a person were only fitting. This made me shrink again, but I couldn't give in now. One hundred and twenty eyes were watching me.

"Who are you fellows?"

"I'm in charge of sports; he keeps the classroom nice."

"So, what's up?"

"Om Sokdae, our class monitor . . . didn't he ask you to come over?"

Hearing for the second time that his name was Om Sokdae, that he was monitor, and that for this one reason I had to present myself and wait on his command, did begin to make me feel intimidated.

My experience of monitors in Seoul was that the job never had anything to do with physical strength. Sometimes monitors were appointed because they came from well-to-do families, or because they were good at sports and, as a result, popular. But usually the selection of the monitor was based on exam scores and, apart from a certain prestige that went with the job, it amounted to no more than being a messenger between the students and the teacher. On those rare occasions when the appointee was physically strong, strength was almost never used to repress the others or to force them to do menial tasks. This wasn't just because of the next monitor election; the children themselves wouldn't put up with it. That day, however, I met a completely new kind of monitor.

"If the monitor calls, is that it? Do we have to run to him on call and wait on his commands?" I demanded, making a final stand with the resolve of a true Seoulite.

I couldn't understand what happened next. The words were hardly out of my lips when the boys looking on suddenly burst out laughing. More than fifty boys guffawed, including the two who had been giving me a hard time and even Om Sokdae. I was at a complete loss. When I had regained enough control to begin to wonder what I had said that had caused such hilarity, the boy who was in charge of keeping the classroom tidy choked back his laughter and asked, "You mean you don't come when the monitor calls? What sort of school did you go to? Where was it? Didn't you have a class monitor?"

What happened next was a freakish shift in my consciousness. Suddenly, I had the feeling that I was doing something very wrong, that I was holding out in defiance of a teacher after he had called on me. This overwhelming illusion of deliberate refusal to give in to a teacher may have been produced by the boys' nonstop shrieks of laughter.

As I approached Om Sokdae hesitantly, his boisterous laughter changed to a nice, pleasant smile.

"Is it that difficult to come over for a minute?" he asked.

His voice was different now, coated with affection. I was so moved by this gentleness that I almost jumped up and nodded my head. But I still felt a certain antagonism, even though it had slipped down to the lowest level of consciousness. This feeling prevented me from doing anything quite so undignified.

Om Sokdae was an extraordinary boy. In a brief moment, not only did he wash clean any feeling I had of being brought to him against my will, but he then freed me from my disappointment in the behavior of our teacher.

"What school did you say you went to in Seoul? How big is it? A terrific school, I suppose? Our school wouldn't compare at all, would it?"

By asking these questions he gave me an opportunity to boast about my Seoul school: I was able to tell him that there were more than twenty classes in third grade, that the school had tradition stretching back almost sixty years, that in this year's entrance exam more than ninety students had gotten into Kyonggi Middle School.

"How about your exam scores? Where were you in your class? What else are you good at?" he asked, giving me an opportunity to boast that in fourth grade I had won the top prize in Korean (our school at this time was already giving top prizes in each individual subject), and that the previous year I had won the top award at a children's art contest in Kyongbok Palace.

This wasn't all. It was almost as if Sokdae could read my heart. He asked me about my father's job and our family circumstances. As a result, without any impression of putting on undue airs, I was able to tell the others my father ranked next to the county manager in the local administration and that we lived comfortably with a radio and three clocks including the pendulum clock on the wall.

"Good . . . Well, let's see . . ."

Sokdae folded his arms like an adult, giving me the impression that he had something in mind. He pointed to a desk in the row in front of his own.

"You sit there," he said. "That's your place."

I was a bit taken aback.

"The teacher told me to sit back there," I said, suddenly remembering how things were in Seoul, but no longer feeling the same combative spirit I'd felt just a few moments ago. Sokdae let my objection pass as if he hadn't heard.

"Hey, Kim Yongsu, change places here with Han Pyongt'ae."

At Sokdae's bidding the boy gathered his things into his bag without a word. The absolute obedience of the boy overwhelmed me once again. I hesitated for a moment, but thinking my hesitation might be construed as resistance, I changed places.

There were at least two other things that day that really boggled my mind. One of them happened at lunchtime. When my conversation with Sokdae was over, he put his lunchbox up on the desk. This was the signal for everyone to open their lunchboxes. Five or six in the group proceeded to bring things over to Sokdae. Among the things they put on his desk were some steamed sweet potatoes and eggs, roasted peanuts, and some apples. Finally, one boy in the front row poured some water into a porcelain cup and placed that too, respectfully, on Sokdae's desk. Everyone behaved as they would to the teacher on a picnic. Sokdae accepted everything without a single word of thanks. The most he did was give a little smile to the boy who had brought the eggs.

The second thing happened during the break after the fifth period when two boys in the section of the class next to me got into a fight and one of them got a bloody nose. Immediately, the boys who were looking on went to find Sokdae, who had left the classroom before the fight broke out. It was just like Seoul children going for the teacher when they encountered something they could not handle. The way Sokdae handled the affair when he returned was not very different from the way a teacher would. He stuffed the boy's bleeding nose with a wad of cotton wool from the first-aid box. Then he got him to hold his head back. He slapped the boy who had caused the nosebleed and made him kneel down on the dais with his arms raised. Both boys followed Sokdae's directives quietly as if it were all perfectly normal. Even more strange was the teacher's attitude when he came in for the sixth period. After listening quietly to Sokdae's report, he took the stick that was used to clean the blackboard duster and gave the offender several hard slaps across the palms. In this way, the teacher endorsed what seemed to me to be flagrantly inappropriate behavior on Sokdae's part.

When I came home from school that day, I began again to examine carefully this new order and environment. A certain mental paralysis, the result of being thrown suddenly into a very strange school environment, and a feeling of being threatened by the rigidity of this new order, which now suddenly was weighing down on me, filled my head with a kind of fog; everything was so fuzzy that I couldn't think.

Although at twelve it's still easy enough to treat everything with the innocence of a child, I had the feeling I wouldn't be able to transfer into this new order and environment. What had happened violated completely the principles of reason and freedom by which I had been reared all my life. I had not yet experienced directly the full brunt of Sokdae's order, but I had more than a vague presentiment of the irrationality and violence I would have to endure after accepting it. It all seemed like a horrible prearranged plan that was destined to become reality.

However, the prospect of fighting was dreary beyond belief. Where would I begin, who would I have to fight, and how would the fight be conducted?—it was all so daunting. It was clear that there was something wrong, that there was enormous injustice in a system founded on irrationality and violence. But it was too much to expect me at that time to have either a concrete understanding or a concrete response. To tell the truth, even today at forty, I don't have the complete confidence needed to handle this sort of thing.

Not having a brother, I told my father about Sokdae. I wanted to describe what I had had to put up with from Sokdae that day and get advice about what I should do in the future. But my father's reaction was unexpected. I had barely finished describing Sokdae's strange behavior and was just about to ask a question in the hope of getting advice when Father suddenly said in a voice filled with wonder, "That boy is really something. You said his name was Om Sokdae, didn't you? If he's like that already, he's surely heading for great things."

Obviously Father didn't recognize the existence of any injustice here at all. Hot under the collar now, I told my father about the monitor system in

Seoul. I described how things were decided reasonably by election and that no restraints were put on our freedom. But Father seemed to interpret my attachment to reason and freedom purely as a sign of weakness.

"What a weakling you are! Why do you always have to be in the crowd? Why do you believe *you* can't be monitor? Think of how things would be if you were monitor yourself. What better example could you have of what a monitor should do?"

He went on then to advocate fixing my sights on the monitor's job, which Om Sokdae now held, telling me not to be angry at the unfortunate situation the class found itself in, nor at the system that had created this situation, nor at the bad management of the system.

Poor Dad! It's only now that I think I understand him and the bitter taste of humiliation, the sense of powerlessness he was experiencing after being tossed from a plum job in the central office in Seoul and being made section chief of general affairs in the county administration. He had been nailed by an overzealous boss for staying at his desk and not rushing out to greet the minister when the latter came on inspection. He must have had a greater thirst for power now than at any other time in his life. But he had always been the one who believed in reason, the one who scolded my mother for caring more about my ability to go out and give some boy a beating than about my grades.

Of course, at the time, I had no way of understanding all of this, so my father's abrupt change left me at a complete loss. My confusion was all the greater since, next to my teachers, my father had always had the greatest influence on my decisions. As a result, instead of learning how to deal with the impending fight, I was left confused about the very existence of the injustice itself, and this was crucial in deciding whether or not a fight was necessary.

Still, I listened attentively to my father's advice, and as soon as I got to school the next day, I began to examine the possibilities. Father's advice, however, was quite impracticable. Unlike in Seoul, where an election for class monitor took place every term, I was told there wouldn't be an election here until the spring. There was no way of knowing how the class would be divided then. And even if I prepared for the election, someone like me, who had drifted in suddenly in fifth grade, had little or no chance of winning. Even if it were possible to win, the thought of the humiliation the other children and I would have to endure in the meantime was like a nightmare. In addition, Om Sokdae did not wait for me to prepare at my leisure for next year.

Our little clash that first day, even though it ended in my surrender, made a strong impression on Om Sokdae. It seemed to put him on his guard. Perhaps not quite sure of his victory the first day, he tried to confirm it the next day. Again it was at lunchtime. I had just taken the lid off my lunchbox when a boy in the row in front of me looked back and said, "It's your turn today. Fetch Om Sokdae a cup of water. Then you can have your lunch."

"What?"

I had raised my voice without being aware of it.

"Are you deaf? Bring over a cup of water. We don't want food to stick in the monitor's throat, do we? It's your turn today."

"Who decided whose turn it was? Why do we have to fetch water for the monitor? Is the monitor a teacher or what? Doesn't the monitor have any hands or feet?" I countered loudly, outraged. In

Seoul, an errand like that would be considered an insufferable insult. It took an enormous effort on my part to stop myself from using foul language. Still, my bluntness made the boy hesitate. Suddenly, from behind my back, Om Sokdae's familiar voice said threateningly, "Hey, Han Pyongt'ae, cut it out and fetch a cup of water."

"No. I won't."

I greeted Sokdae with a stony refusal. I was so angry I didn't even see him. He slammed the lid roughly on his lunchbox and walked over toward me, his face set in anger.

"I'll have to do something about you, you little *sekki*," he shouted threateningly, his eyes wide and his fists raised. "So you refuse to fetch the water?"

He seemed determined to force me to submit. Intimidated by this flash of temper—it seemed as if one of those big fists might strike out at any time—I got up abruptly. But I just couldn't run that errand. I hesitated for a moment. Suddenly, I had an idea.

"Fine. I'll just ask the teacher first, then I'll fetch you the water. I'll ask him whether a classmate has to fetch water for the monitor."

I strode off as soon as I had finished. I was staking everything on my sense that he was constantly careful to make a good impression on the teacher. Even I was surprised by the effect.

"Stop!" Sokdae shouted before I had gone more than a few steps. Then he added in a roar, "All right. Forget it. I don't need water from a *sekki* like you anyway."

At first glance it seemed like a splendid victory. In fact, it was the beginning of a lonely, tedious fight that continued for the next six months.

Since Sokdae had run the class for the last year with little or no opposition, I must have really been a thorn in his side. My action that day must have seemed more than simple resistance; he must have read it as a serious challenge. At the same time, it was obvious that, if he had a mind to, he could take care of me in any number of ways. I mean, he had the legitimate power of monitor conferred on him by the teacher, and he also had the best fists in the grade.

But so far from again brandishing a fist in anger, he didn't even show any hostility directly toward me. When he used his authority from the teacher to conduct checks on homework assignments or on cleaning chores, he didn't use it to discriminate against me. Looking back on it now, he showed an eerie composure and precision quite unexpected in a young boy.

Persecution and discrimination invariably and only came when Sokdae stood some distance away. Boys who didn't appear to be at all friendly with Sokdae picked fights with me over trifling things. And when the class ganged up on me to give me a hard time or to make fun of me, Sokdae was never present. It was just the same when they excluded me from their games, showing an unwarranted hostility, or when they stopped talking if I approached a group who were gabbing boisterously. Sokdae was obviously behind it, but he never seemed to be around. Then there was the question of information, something that's vital to children even if adults consider it unimportant. For example, where the peddler had set up, where the circus had pitched their tent, when there was a bullfight scheduled for the stadium, when the Culture Center was showing a free movie on the bank of the river—this sort of information. I was always left out. This, too, on the face of it, was quite unrelated to Sokdae.

In fact, when Sokdae did come to me, it was very often in the role of savior or problem-solver. When I was sweating over some boy who was picking on me, someone I wouldn't be able to beat in a fight, Sokdae was the one who came on the scene and prevented the fight from taking place. And it was because of Sokdae that, after due isolation, I was allowed to join in the games of the others.

However, Sokdae's composure and clinical precision was matched by the sharpness of my own awareness of what was going on. From the beginning, I was aware intuitively of an invisible cord tying the persecution meted out by the boys to my deliverance by Sokdae. I had a cold inner awareness that it was all a trick to get me under his control. As a result, the deliverance he dispensed, rather than filling me with thanks, made me tremble with shame. On each successive occasion, the fire of enmity, burning in my heart at a new level of intensity, provided me with the strength to endure the long, difficult fight afterwards.

When it comes to a fight, the first victory a twelve year old thinks about is the kind that comes from physical strength. But in my fight with

Sokdae, there was no possibility of this. Sokdae was a head taller than me and equivalently stronger. From what I had heard, his family registration was wrong; although he was in the same grade as us, he was two or three years older. In addition, he was an uncommonly skilled fighter. By the time he was in fourth grade, he was fast enough and intrepid enough to whip a middle-school student.

Accordingly, the first thing I tried was to drive a wedge between Sokdae and the boys in the class, all of whom were on his side. In particular, there were three or four boys, all about the same size as Sokdae, who sat in the back of the class. I concentrated on them, figuring that if I drove a wedge there, I might be able, with their help, to take on Sokdae. Braving tongue-lashings from my mother for using an excessive amount of pocket money, I was able to buy their favor temporarily, but the effort to drive a wedge between Sokdae and them failed every time. Things would be going along nicely and I seemed to be winning a little favor, but as soon as I said something calculated to turn them against Sokdae, their faces would set tensely, and from the next day they would begin to avoid me.

They seemed to have an instinctual terror of Sokdae.

When I think about it now, my failure was as much due to my mistakes as Sokdae's leadership qualities. Even in children's minds there had to be something that reacted to the adult aspiration toward justice and freedom. But instead of trying to awaken these boys to a great cause or persuade them to support it, I let myself be swayed by my own personal feelings and quick temper. I concentrated on buying an immediate gain. The only thing missing was the sort of low-down, sly, political trickery that goes hand in hand with adult campaigning.

However, my most decisive defeat in the fight with Sokdae came in the area of schoolwork, an area in which I had been quietly confident. From the beginning of the fight, I had figured on being able to floor Sokdae with my exam marks. For a month I had been looking forward to the regular exam in mid-April: It presented a ready-made opportunity.

I had reason for confidence in this area. The colossal difference between the Seoul school and this school indicated that taking first place should be easy. In addition, Sokdae didn't appear to study much. Even now I have the habit of sizing people up in terms of mind and matter and usually I am right.

I waited for the exam, counting the days, but the results were quite unexpected. Sokdae scored an average of 98.5, first in the class of course, but also in the entire grade. With a score of 92.6, I barely managed to get second in the class, and I wasn't in the first ten in the grade. Although the difference was not quite as great as in the matter of fists, still I was no real match for him. In the face of such a clear outcome, there was no point in being suspicious of his academic success or in being angry.

Nevertheless I gave myself to that hopeless fight, swept up by a dark, strange zeal I couldn't understand. I had no hope with fists, with creating sides, or with study, so I turned my eye now to Sokdae's weakness—I was sure he had been taking advantage of the others. I turned very early to the original tactic used by adults in fights when all else has failed: the strategy of uncovering and spreading ugly rumors.

I began to dig into Sokdae's misdeeds so that, first, I could use the information to drive a wedge between him and the teacher. I knew that the trust he enjoyed with the teacher was as much a part of his power as his skill in fighting. The teacher's blind trust, which gave Sokdae authority to police clean-up chores, to check homework assignments, even to dispense punishment, provided a legitimate framework for his violence and allowed him to reign so powerfully over us.

However, uncovering Sokdae's misdeeds didn't prove easy. Judging from the repressive atmosphere in the class and the dark crushed faces of the boys, I figured all I had to do was a little digging and his crimes would all spill out, but I failed to find anything worth talking about. Clearly he beat the boys and abused them, but almost always he had the excuse that he was acting with the teacher's approval. Although he ate their snacks and used their things without giving any recompense, the boys invariably had offered the stuff freely.

The more I examined Sokdae, the more clearly I saw that the teacher's reasons for trusting him were, in a sense, verified time after time. Our class under Sokdae was a model for the whole school. His fists were more effective than the perfunctory disciplinary control of any on-duty teacher or sixth-grade prefect in keeping the boys from eating sweets or breaking any other petty school regulation. With Sokdae in charge of clean-up chores, he made sure we had the cleanest classroom in the school, and he kept our flower bed eye-catchingly bright. With Sokdae overseeing our planting project, we recorded the best results in the school. His system of enforced allocation meant our class had more perks than any other class. For example, the walls were crammed to overflowing with expensive frames. With him as captain, our team won every contest with other classes. In acting as a leader in all things, he imitated the grown-up strategy of "I'll pay so much . . ." so that he concluded projects faster and better than when the teachers directed the children personally. And though it was no big deal, by controlling the entire grade with his fists, he ensured that no boy in our class got beaten by a boy from some other class. None of this could have been displeasing to our teacher either.

Notwithstanding all this, I continued to fight with a passion that came from treacherous intent; the more hopeless the prospect, the more I burned with a strange tenacity. I directed my eyes and ears totally to Sokdae in an effort to dig out his misdeeds.

Even now I don't understand Sokdae's attitude toward me. About three months had gone by since I had transferred in, and presumably the others had told him about my efforts to get to him, but his attitude never changed. Far from showing any dislike for the way I was opposing him, he didn't even show any sign of impatience. It was an extraordinary forbearance, unexplainable by the few years difference in our ages. If it weren't for my passion and obstinacy, I would have given in to him by this stage.

However, there's profit in waiting; my time finally came. It must have been around the middle of June because the white acacia were in bloom along the road to school. Yun Pyongjo, whose father was a dry cleaner, had brought something special to school, and he was bragging about it to the boys in the class. It was an expensive gold-plated lighter, the kind we used to call the "round lighter." The lighter caused a minor commotion as it went from hand to hand around the class. Sokdae, who had been out for a minute, saw it as soon as he returned. He came up close, reached out his hand, and said, "Give us a look."

The boys, until that moment boisterously laughing and voicing their admiration, fell silent immediately. The lighter passed into Sokdae's hand. Sokdae examined it for a while.

"Whose is it?" he asked Pyongjo expressionlessly.

"My father's," Pyongjo answered, his voice reduced to a crawling whisper. Sokdae lowered his voice a little, too.

"Did you get it from him?" he asked.

"No, I just took it to school."

"Who knows you took it?"

"No one except my brother."

A faint smile flickered around Sokdae's mouth. He began to examine the lighter carefully.

"Yah, it's lovely," Sokdae finally said, holding the lighter firmly in his hand and looking intently at Pyongjo.

I had been watching Sokdae carefully from the beginning. I tensed suddenly at this new development. From my experience in watching Sokdae, I knew that when he said this, he meant something different than people usually mean. When Sokdae wanted something belonging to one of the others, his "Yah, it's lovely" meant he was asking for it. Usually this was enough for the item to be handed over. But sometimes a boy might hold out a bit and then Sokdae would say, "Lend it to me." Of course he meant, "Hand it over!" No one could stand up to this, and the item invariably went over. This was the secret of how Sokdae never "took" things from the others but always "got" them. Not having any way of conceptualizing silent coercion, I had always taken these "donations" as relatively blameless, but today I saw that his action barely had even the minimum camouflage.

Predictably Pyongjo put on a tearful face that indicated he couldn't comply.

"Give it back," he said firmly. "I've got to return it to its place before my father comes back."

"Where did your father go?" Sokdae asked quietly, ignoring Pyongjo's outstretched hand.

"Seoul. He'll be back tomorrow."

"I see . . ." Sokdae said, dragging out the final vowel and examining the lighter again. Suddenly, something must have occurred to him, and he shot a glance back at me. I had been watching carefully, hoping he'd make a decisive mistake, but I flinched now beneath his sudden gaze. His gaze somehow seemed to say I was a nuisance; at the same time, it had a hidden glint of anger, and this may have made me flinch all the more. However, it was just for a moment. With an air of total unconcern, he handed the lighter back to Pyongjo.

"It's not on then . . . I wish I could have borrowed it," he said. I was very disappointed when Sokdae surrendered the lighter so easily. Those eyes glued to the lighter as he rubbed it and examined it clearly revealed no minor feeling of coveting. To be able to control himself so easily and turn aside his desire filled me with a renewed sense of fear.

However, ultimately Sokdae too had his own limitations. On the way home from school that day I noticed that Pyongjo was behaving quite differently from the way he had that morning. He wore a worried expression, and as the boys clamored out the school gate, he walked with drooping shoulders a few steps behind the rest. Immediately I knew why.

We lived in the same part of town and could easily have gone together, but I was determined to follow him at a little distance. This was because I felt Sokdae's eyes watching from some place of concealment. It was only when I saw all the others branch off along the way for their own parts of town, leaving Pyongjo walking leaden footed and alone, that I quickened my footsteps. In a moment I was right beside him.

"Hey, Yun Pyongjo!" I called.

Pyongjo had been walking very slowly, buried deep in thought. Shocked out of his reverie, he looked back.

"Sokdae took the lighter from you, didn't he?" I asked straight out, without giving him any chance.

"He didn't actually take it . . . I lent it to him."

"That means he took it, doesn't it? And isn't your father due back tomorrow?"

"I'll just tell my brother not to say anything."

"You mean you'll steal your father's lighter and give it to Sokdae. Your father won't mind losing such a fine lighter?"

Pyongjo's face twisted, reaching a new level of darkness. "I'm worried. The lighter was a present to my father from my uncle in Japan."

Finally Pyongjo let it out. And with a sigh quite

out of character for a child, he added, "What can I do? Sokdae wants it."

"You lent it, didn't you? You can always get back what you lend, can't you?" I asked sarcastically because I resented Pyongjo's absurd resignation. But the poor boy was so buried in his own worries he wasn't even aware of my sarcasm: He took what I said at face value.

"He won't give it back."

"Is that so? And you call that lending? You mean he took it."

There was silence.

"Don't be a fool . . . why not tell the teacher? That's better than catching it from your father, isn't it?"

"I can't do that!"

Pyongjo's voice suddenly got loud. He shook his head firmly to show that he was absolutely determined. I had once more come up against an area in the psychology of the boys that I did not really understand.

"Are you *that* afraid of Sokdae?"

I figured this was one time I could establish this definitely one way or another, so I appealed to his personal pride. It was a waste of time. Although there was a blue flash in his eyes from sudden humiliation, his answer was absolutely firm.

"You don't know, so stay out of it."

However, the affair wasn't totally without profit. Pyongjo walked on in silence, his lips closed tight as a clam after what I'd said. I kept following him, picking at him, and I established beyond a doubt that the lighter had been taken by Sokdae, not lent to him. This was really great since I was looking for proof of one of Sokdae's misdeeds.

As soon as I got to school next day I went to the faculty room and found our teacher. With very little sense of doing something cowardly I told the teacher about the Yun Pyongjo affair and all the similar stories I had seen myself or heard about since coming to the school. Although, doubtless, this was a clear display of Seoul-style sycophancy, still the teacher's reaction was unexpected.

"What's that? Are you certain of what you're saying?"

I could read clearly in the teacher's expression that he found the whole thing a nuisance. Annoyed by his lack of outrage, I began to enumerate

Sokdae's other misdeeds, things that were still pure conjecture. The teacher showed no inclination to listen to me at all, and his irritation showed in his voice as he got rid of me.

"All right, all right," he said. "Go on back. I'll see about it in a minute."

I felt I couldn't rely on the teacher. At the same time I waited for class to start with a certain amount of anticipation since he said he would investigate the matter. However, something happened in the free study period just before morning assembly that changed everything. A messenger boy came to the door at the back, beckoned Sokdae, and whispered something to him. The boy had completed school about two years ago and had stayed on as a messenger. I began to feel uneasy as soon as I saw him. I remembered that when I was recounting Sokdae's misdeeds to the teacher, he was standing not far away copying something at the mimeograph machine.

As you might expect, Sokdae came back to his place, spent a moment in thought, took the lighter out of his pocket, and crossed over to Yun Pyongjo.

"Your father is coming back today, right? Okay.

Give this back to him," he said, handing back the lighter to Pyongjo. Then in a louder voice he added, "I just took charge of it for a while in case you'd cause a fire or something. Children shouldn't play with things like that."

He said it loud enough for the entire class to hear. At first Pyongjo was at a complete loss, but soon his face brightened.

Not quite five minutes later, the teacher stepped into the classroom, his face grimmer than usual.

"Om Sokdae!" the teacher called as soon as he reached the podium.

Sokdae answered and got up very calmly. The teacher reached out his hand.

"Bring the lighter here," he said.

"What?"

"Yun Pyongjo's father's lighter."

Without the slightest change in expression, Sokdae replied, "I gave it back to Pyongjo already. I just took charge of it in case he'd accidentally start a fire while playing with it."

"What did you say?"

The teacher shot an angry glance at me, but to confirm the information he called Yun Pyongjo.

"Is Om Sokdae telling the truth? Where is the lighter?"

"Yes, I have it here," Pyongjo answered quickly.

I was completely dumfounded. I stood there like an idiot, not knowing how to begin to explain this sudden reversal of circumstances. I heard the teacher calling my name.

"What's going on here?" he asked. He wasn't really asking a question; he was telling me off. I leapt to my feet and shouted, "He gave it back before you came in."

My voice shook because I knew the teacher wouldn't believe me.

"Hold your tongue! All this fuss about nothing . . ." the teacher said, cutting me short. I never got a chance to tell him the messenger boy had warned Sokdae. Actually there was no proof the messenger boy had told Sokdae.

The teacher continued to ignore me. He turned to the class.

"Is it true that Om Sokdae is giving you a hard time?" he asked. "Have any of you had to put up with that sort of thing?"

The faces of the children instantly set strangely. Seeing this, the teacher, with a pretense of real concern, this time asked softly, "You can say whatever you like here. You don't have to be afraid of Om Sokdae. Speak out. Where and what was taken, who was hit without doing anything wrong . . . tell me . . . anyone?"

No one raised a hand or got up; no one even wavered. Aware of a strange sense of relief among the boys, the teacher continued to look at them for some time.

"Is there no one?" he asked once again. "From what I've been given to understand, there should be quite a few."

"No one!"

About half the class, centering on the group around Sokdae, shouted in response. The teacher's face lightened a full shade. Reassured, he repeated the question.

"Are you sure? There was really nothing like that?

"No, nothing."

This time all the children, with the exception of Sokdae and me, shouted at the top of their voices.

"All right then. We can start morning assembly."

The teacher, having disposed of the matter as if he had known the outcome from the beginning, opened the roll book. Fortunately he didn't single me out in front of the others to scold me; he was content to believe Sokdae and the class and let it go at that.

Eventually class began. Stunned as I was by this sudden reversal, there was no way I could concentrate on what the teacher was saying. All I was aware of was the strange buzz of Sokdae's voice reverberating inside my head, fielding and answering all the teacher's questions with a note of triumph. The first class was over when finally the teacher's voice registered with me.

"Han Pyongt'ae, I'll see you for a minute in the faculty room," the teacher said as he went out, making an effort to appear calm. I figured, looking at his back, that he was very angry. I got up mechanically from my desk and followed him.

"Bloody *sekki*, he's just a tattletale." Words filled with hostility seemed to pierce my eardrums.

The teacher was puffing continuously on his cigarette to cool down his anger.

"Telling tales is wrong. More than that, you told a lie," he said, reprimanding me as soon as I went in. Perhaps he took my silence, which was due to my total bewilderment, as an admission of guilt, because he added, "I had high hopes for you, coming from Seoul and being a good student, but I have to say I'm very disappointed. I've had this class for two years. We never had anything like this before. It scares me to think that our innocent children will turn out like you!"

I was angry enough when I left the classroom, but now the finality of the teacher's reprimand made me almost scream. The sudden awareness of the seriousness of the crisis saved me from confusion. If I couldn't straighten this whole thing out, it really would be the end. Sunk in despair, I made frantic efforts to pull myself together.

"The messenger boy told Sokdae what I had told you. When Sokdae heard this . . . just before you came in . . ."

I groped for the words to say what I had been unable to say in the classroom.

"What about the others? Didn't all sixty agree there was nothing like that?"

The teacher must have been amazed at my obstinacy. By this time, as I said, I was frantic.

"The others are afraid of Om Sokdae."

"That's precisely why I asked two or three times."

"But it was in front of Om Sokdae."

"Are you saying they're more afraid of Sokdae than they are of me."

An idea flashed into my mind.

"Call them one by one when Sokdae isn't there, then ask them, or get them to write it out without signing their names. I'm sure Om Sokdae's misdeeds will spill out."

I was so filled with conviction, I shouted my reply. The other teachers, thinking something strange was going on, stole sidelong glances at us.

The basis of my conviction was that when I was in Seoul, I had seen the teachers use this method from time to time to solve problems that seemed otherwise quite insoluble. For example, they used this method to find something when we didn't know when or where the article had been lost.

"Now you want to turn all sixty into informers," the teacher said, turning to the other teachers with a sigh as if the whole thing was quite beyond him. A teacher beside us glared at me and chimed in.

"The Seoul teachers obviously did things they shouldn't with the children."

I couldn't understand for the life of me how the method I had proposed could be so interpreted. They were all on Sokdae's side; I can't put into words how angry I was that they put a bad interpretation on whatever I said. Suddenly I had an awful feeling of suffocation and tears began to pour out uncontrollably.

The tears had an unexpected effect. As I stood there blubbering, tears streaming from my eyes, the teacher looked up at me in surprise. After a little interval, he stubbed out his cigarette on the corner of the desk and said quietly, "All right, Han Pyongt'ae, we'll try it your way once more. Go on back now."

His face revealed that he had finally reached some awareness of the gravity of the problem.

Not wanting to look bad before the others, I washed away the tear marks. When I got back to the classroom, the atmosphere was strange. This was a free period and the boys should have been romping around. Instead the classroom was as quiet as if they were getting a special demonstration lesson. Thinking this strange, I looked toward the teacher's podium, where all eyes were directed: Om Sokdae was standing there. I don't know what he had just been saying, but when I got into the classroom, he looked at the children and brandished his fist high in the air. You understand, don't you? he seemed to say.

The teacher came in for the next period, rustling a sheaf of papers. Om Sokdae called, "Attention! Salute!" Immediately afterwards, the teacher called Sokdae.

"Class monitor," he said, "go down to the faculty room. On my desk you'll find the chart for the class savings program I've been working on. Finish it off for me. All you have to do is mark in the lines in red; I've done the rest."

When Sokdae had gone out, the teacher spoke to the boys in a tone of voice quite different than he had used in the earlier period.

"In this period we have to deal with the Om Sokdae problem. There were some mistakes with the way I asked the questions in the last period. I'm going to ask again. Has there been any problem between you and Om Sokdae? This time, however, you don't have to raise your hand, or stand up, or shout anything out. Don't sign your name, just write down on the exam paper whatever it was he did to you. I understand that many of you were beaten without any reason and that many more had school things and money taken. Anything like that, no matter how small, just write it down here. This is not like tattling or talking about someone behind his back. We're doing this for the class and for yourselves, so there's no need to be watching the reaction of others. You mustn't discuss the matter or interfere with anyone in any way. I'll be responsible for what happens. I'll protect you."

He handed out a blank sheet to each of the children.

I felt the disappointment and resentment I had entertained toward the teacher melt away. I've got Sokdae now, I thought, and I wrote down all his misdeeds that I knew about.

After writing for a while, I turned around to discover I was the only one writing busily. All the rest were just looking furtively at each other. They didn't even have pencils in their hands.

Before long the teacher seemed to realize, too, what was happening. After a moment's thought, he freed them from the last rein that bound them. They had been rendered powerless by Sokdae's invisible spies mingled among them.

"I seem to have made another mistake. It's not just Om Sokdae's personal faults that I want to know. I want to know all the problems in the class. So, it doesn't have to be about Om Sokdae. Whoever, whatever—anyone that's done anything wrong—write it down on the page. Anyone who knowingly conceals the fault of a classmate could be regarded as worse than the perpetrator of the fault."

After the teacher had spoken like this, a few of the boys took up their pencils. I relaxed when I saw this. Now all Sokdae's misdeeds, for so long concealed, would be revealed. In this conviction I filled the rest of the answer sheet with Sokdae's sins, regarding as proved many things I had till then hesitated over as mere conjecture.

Finally the bell rang for the end of class. The

teacher gathered up the sheets he had handed out and left the classroom without a word. He didn't as much as glance at anyone on the way out, as if to say he had no preconceived ideas.

I waited for the results with a quiet sense of anticipation. Irrespective of whatever Sokdae had said to the other boys while I was out of the classroom, I firmly believed all Sokdae's sins would be brought to light without fail this time.

The teacher was about ten minutes late coming into the classroom for the next period, perhaps because he had to read all our unsigned indictments. However, he went directly into classwork without revealing a word of what he had read.

Next period was the same and the period after that. The teacher went on with classwork as if nothing had happened. During class his eyes met mine from time to time, but he gave me no particular indication one way or another. It wasn't until after final assembly that the teacher called me.

For more than two hours already I had been gripped by terrible anxiety. When Sokdae first heard from the others what had gone on in the class during his absence, his face had been noticeably dark. During the third and fourth periods, he still looked dejected. After lunch he changed abruptly. Once again he returned to his old, arrogant, full-of-himself attitude, from time to time throwing glances at me that seemed to imply I deserved to be pitied. This was what triggered my anxiety.

"Take a look at this first," the teacher said, handing me the bunch of unsigned indictments as soon as I had reluctantly entered the faculty room. My hand shook as I went through them one at a time. Half were blank, notwithstanding the teacher's repeated instructions. The real surprise was the content of the half that had something written on them.

To give the precise figures, fifteen of thirty-two revealed my misdeeds: buying sweets on the way to and from school; going into comic stores; leaving school not through the main gate, but through a hole in the barbed wire fence at the back; kicking the bamboo supports in someone's cucumber patch; pulling hairs from the rump of the horse tied below the bridge—all the petty offenses a boy might commit were arrayed more neatly there than I could actually remember them. Time after time it popped up that I had said the teacher was shabbier and dumber than my Seoul teacher. And then there was the embarrassing report about Yunhei, a girl whom I had played with several times. She was a sixth-grader who lived next door.

Next after me came a boy by the name of Kim Yonggi who was a bit slow-witted. The five or six misdemeanors attributed to him were due more to lack of brains than bad behavior. Then came Lee Huido from the orphanage with three or four and someone with two or three. The staggering thing was Om Sokdae. My paper was the only one that said anything about him.

After I finished reading, I felt more than anger. It was as if I had fallen into a bottomless pit, or rather, as if a big, high wall stood right in front of my nose, blocking me, and I was dizzy and hopelessly lost. The teacher's voice circled around my ears as if it were sprinkling words in the distant sky.

"I think I understand . . . you were dissatisfied with everything. So completely different here . . . to the Seoul way of doing things. Especially Om Sokdae's way of doing things as monitor . . . in a way you could call it not good . . . and coarse too. But that's the way it is here. I know there are schools with student councils, where everything is decided by discussion and vote . . . where the monitor is only a messenger boy. I suppose . . . in Seoul where all the children are bright . . . that's probably the way to run a class. But just because it's fine there, it doesn't follow that it's fine everywhere. We have our own way here and it's up to you to adapt to it. You have to give up thinking that the Seoul way is unconditionally good and our way unconditionally bad. Even if you insist you are right . . . at least, you have to change your approach. You can't fight with everyone in the class who won't join you, and you can't just spin around on your own like oil in water. You saw it today, didn't you? Not one in the sixty was on your side. If you wanted to remove Om Sokdae as monitor . . . to make our class like your class in Seoul . . . the first thing you had to do was get your classmates on your side. Maybe you'll say you couldn't because Om Sokdae had them in the palm of his hand, but you should have got the children on your side before you came running to me. That wasn't possible, you may say, so you came to me . . . and you think as teacher it was my job to fix it since the children are stupid . . . but you're wrong. Even if you're right . . . with all the children in the class supporting Sokdae, I have no choice but to support him. And even if, as you are completely convinced, the support of the children is false, based on Sokdae's intimidation and wiles . . . it's still the same. I have to respect the power the children have given Sokdae. Up until now our class has presented a solid united front . . . you can't break that up with vague suspicions. In addition . . . one way or another, Sokdae is the best student in the grade . . . he is a model monitor . . . with real leadership ability . . . don't look at him blindly with biased eyes . . . you have to be able to recognize his strong points too . . . above all you must go back among the boys . . . make a new beginning with them. If you want to compete with Sokdae, compete fairly. Do you understand?"

It seemed as if the teacher would finish at any moment what he had to say, but he kept on going. If he had reprimanded me in a loud voice, I think I would have stood up to him and asserted myself. If he had shown anger on his face or given the slightest indication of disliking me, I don't think I'd have sat on there listening as quietly as I remember having done. His voice and his eyes, so genuinely concerned, seemingly repressing his own feelings, took away from me the strength to resist. Confronted by the strange logic of this cold, unfeeling teacher, I sat on quietly, completely stunned. When I finally got out from there, my mind and body felt like a bit of laundry after it has been wrung dry.

If fighting is considered purely in terms of the will to attack or to defend, my fight with Sokdae ended that day. But if refusal to submit and unwillingness to compromise are regarded as a form of fighting, then my lonely, tedious fight continued for another two months. My genuine conviction, trampled on by the foolish or cowardly mob, turned into a kind of unyielding bitterness and helped me to stick it out.

Although all my schemes had been blocked, the canny Sokdae, from that day on, never appeared directly in the fight against me. The attacks from others, however, were several times more concentrated and intense than before, and school life became several times more agonizing.

Most painful of all were the fist fights that subsequently came my way, without regard for time or occasion. In every class there was a ranking order in fighting, just as there was in study. My strength and tenacity were enough to rank me about thirteenth or fourteenth. Suddenly my ranking began to be ignored. Boys who previously acknowledged I had beaten them began picking fights with me. I mustered all my strength to deal with these challenges. But my ranking began to slip day after day. Against opponents I could easily beat, I began to suffer crushing defeats in the actual fights. Boys who formerly would start to cry or run away in admission of defeat now stood their ground to the end. The crowd who stood around in a lopsided clique, all supporting my opponent, subtly sapped my strength. And when we rolled in a tangle on the ground, very often, with the assistance of an unknown hand, I found myself pinned under my opponent. Within a month of the lighter affair, I was about last in the class in fighting, if you except a few small fry everyone ignored.

The next most painful thing was the problem of friends. A term had gone by since I had transferred in, but I hadn't been able to make a single friend.

Prior to the lighter affair, some of the boys let me play if I made a special effort. I suppose five or six of them had come home with me at one time or another. After the lighter affair, none of my classmates would have anything to do with me, not just in the school, but also in the local neighborhood. The earlier cold-shouldering paled in comparison to this isolation.

There were no children's playgrounds like there are today, nor were there TV or electronic games to enable you to endure on your own. Something worth reading or even a decent toy were uncommon. It was a huge punishment to have no friends at a time like this. Even now, thoughts of the playtime after lunch at school, or before and after class, bring a shiver to my heart. Unable to participate in any of the games, all I did was stand at the classroom window or in a shady corner of the playground and watch sadly from a distance the teams playing. How wonderful soccer seemed when played with a rubber ball barely the size of an infant's head! Then there was a sort of softball game without a bat, and the figure-eight game with the children screaming in such delight that it seemed as if all their teeth would spill out.

Back home, things weren't any better. In my neighborhood, the range of choice was very limited. I could get the cold-shoulder treatment by associating with boys from other classes who seemed as far removed from me as foreigners; I could tag along with older boys as a rank and filer; or I could gather a crowd of younger boys and play the role of leader, for which I had little stomach. The only other choices were to bury myself in the back room of the comic book store, or rip my mother's lungs inside out by fighting with my brother, who was four years younger.

I remember once a transfer student in the class beside us, bigger and stronger than Sokdae, was taking Sokdae on in a fight after school in the pine grove beside the school. The whole class went to support Sokdae. I went along, too, to support Sokdae, I suppose, because I was a member of the class unit. Just for that day the children pretended not to see me, so that for once I was able to be one of them without incident, and that atmosphere continued for a while after the fight ended in a victory for Sokdae. The boys surrounded Sokdae as if greeting a victorious warrior, and one of them suggested that, as Sokdae was covered with sweat and dirt, they should go to a nearby stream and bathe. Everyone agreed and I got in among them quietly. We had just reached the bank of the stream when Sokdae noticed me. He frowned a little and the atmosphere changed abruptly.

"Hey, Han Pyongt'ae! What are you doing here?" said one of the boys quick on the uptake, and with this shot the others began their assault.

"When did you sneak in?"

"Who asked you to cheer?"

Suddenly, my nose began to sting and tears rolled around my eyes. It wasn't completely clear to me then, but I suppose I was tasting the sorrow of the ostracized, the bitter loneliness that goes with alienation.

However, more painful than the crazy backslide of my fight rating or the isolation was the systematic, open persecution. As I mentioned already, just as there are rules to be observed in the adult world, there are also rules to be observed in the world of children. And just as no adult is able to observe all those rules, it is also difficult for a child to observe all the rules. As the saying goes, if you brush someone, there is always dust. Children live from day to day committing innumerable petty offenses that correspond to adult breaches of the law or adult immorality. For not following the counsels or weekly instructions of the principal, for not doing what the teacher said, or what the student council had decided, for not carrying out the entreaties of parents or elders, or for not observing what society considered to be acceptable behavior—for these kinds of offenses, I became the object of the most rigid application of the regulations.

If my nails were a little long, or if I was a few days late getting a haircut, my name went without fail on the list for poor hygiene. If I had a seam burst, or a button fall off, I was punished for uniform violation. You could usually get away with buying sweets on the way to and from school, but I was always caught. And every time I read comics in the secrecy of the back room of the comic book store, the teacher heard about it and I got a reprimand. In a word, I was caught doing the trivial misdemeanors common to all children, but when I did them, they were regarded as enormous crimes, divulged before the others, censured, and recorded in the records of the student council, and I ended up getting a beating from the teacher or being punished by being assigned some such chore as cleaning the toilets. The accuser was always a different party, but Sokdae was undoubtedly behind it all.

Normally Sokdae was authorized by our cold, indifferent teacher to police and punish these sorts of infractions, and whenever there was a complaint, he exercised his authority in a manner that seemed outwardly fair. For example, if some of his close cronies were caught with me, in front of the others he gave us all the same punishment. But when only Sokdae and his cronies knew the punishment was being carried out, I got different treatment, and this really made me grind my teeth. For example, if we were directed to clean the toilets, they were judged to have completed the assignment and sent home after a perfunctory sweeping, but I was made to wash the stains on the floor before I was allowed to go home.

To some extent it's only conjecture, but I figure

that at other times, too, Sokdae misused his legitimate authority to punish me unfairly. There were hygiene checks I had no idea were coming up—but everyone else had been quietly informed the day before. Or there was the day I was walking alongside a horse and wagon on the way to school and caught and tore my clothes on the spike, that day there was a lightning uniform inspection. These are typical examples. As a result, I eventually became known as a troublemaker and a delinquent, not just in the class but throughout the entire grade.

With school life come to this, there was no way I could study properly. Contrary to my firm determination after transferring here to take first place, my grades began to drop by degrees, so that by the end of the term, I was just about at the top of the middle of the class.

Of course, this does not mean that I took it all quietly on the chin. In my own way, I tried with all my strength and used all my wiles to improve the situation. One thing I tried was to mobilize my parents. Once I had completely given up on my teacher, I sought help from my father, unburdening on him the lonely, difficult fight in which I was embroiled. But ineffectuality had twisted Father into something different from what he once was, so that there wasn't much difference between him and the cold, indifferent teacher.

"What sort of fool are you anyway? Who are you asking to do whose work? If you're not strong enough, haven't you stones and sticks? Try to win first by study. And then if the others won't follow you, well . . ."

Because I was very emotional about the situation, I didn't explain it very well. That was part of it. And then presumably Father regarded the affair as one of those insignificant squabbles so common in the world of children. At any rate, in the face of Father's anger, I lost all stomach to say any more.

Mother was the one who strove to understand, who fretted and fussed about it. Having listened to our conversation, she pushed Father fiercely aside and proceeded quietly to pose me a series of questions. She was off to the school at first light. Inwardly I had a ray of hope that Mother would do something, but it turned out to be futile.

"Why are you so petty and so full of envy? And

your grades, how do you explain them? What's wrong with you? And as well as that, you told a lie to your mother . . . I met your teacher today. We talked for two hours. And that child—what's his name—Om Sokdae. I met him too. Such a sweet, open, sensible child. First in the school . . ."

Mother had started to scold me as soon as I got back from school. She kept lecturing me, just like the teacher, for a good half an hour, but I didn't hear a word. The emotion that gripped me then was something beyond despair. Looking back, I feel a sense of satisfaction when I think that even after this I carried on the struggle—for a while.

However, at last there came a day to end the fight. As the term drew toward its end, I was beginning to feel exhausted. The fierce combative spirit, which I had possessed initially, disappeared, and the hate, which had sustained me like some inner avenging spirit, slowly lost its edge. From the beginning of the new term, I waited quietly for a good opportunity to indicate my submission, but the awful thing was that no opportunity readily presented itself.

One reason for this was that though I had fought

long and hard, I had never once taken on Sokdae directly. It was always other boys, or Sokdae's crowd, who picked on me—or else it was a question of the breach of some regulation, or the legitimate exercise of the power Sokdae had by virtue of his office as monitor. Not only did Sokdae never speak to me as an individual, but we never even looked at each other for very long.

As a result of all this, even after I abandoned all intention of resistance, I was still circling miserably on the outer fringes of the class. Finally, an opportunity came. There was a huge clean-up day to prepare for an inspector coming next day. As soon as class was over in the morning, each of us was given clean-up chores. Needless to say, the chores included cleaning the classroom, but they also extended to tending the flower beds and working on various school projects in the playground.

There was a lot to be swept, cleaned, and tidied, so even with a division of labor the tasks were onerous. I got two windows on the flower bed side. They were sliding windows, eight one-foot-square panes on each side, with vertical and horizontal ribs. Multiplied by two, the total number of panes to be cleaned came to thirty-two. By normal standards this was a lot, but in view of the scale of the clean-up, which involved cleaning the wooden floor of the classroom and corridor with a dry cloth and even waxing it with candle grease, I couldn't say my allotment was unfair.

However, the problem began with the teacher. The teachers in the other classes rolled up their sleeves and directed and supervised the clean-up personally. Our teacher, on the other hand, barely managed to exert himself to divide the workload, and then, as usual, he entrusted inspection to Sokdae before taking off himself very early.

If it had been a few weeks before, when I stood in open confrontation with Sokdae, the teacher's irresponsible delegation of authority would have really annoyed me. But on this day I actually welcomed it. I was well aware that to do the work well on this occasion was a way to catch Sokdae's eye. Before I so resented being checked by Sokdae that I used to perform clean-up chores carelessly.

That day I went to a lot of trouble to clean the windows I had been assigned. First, I used a wet cloth to wash encrusted dirt and stains from the glass and sash, and then I wiped off the wet areas with a dry cloth. Next I used newspaper, followed by white exercise paper, breathing on the panes first, to get rid of any remaining dust.

Going to this trouble took a lot of time, so that by the time I had my two windows bright and shining, most of the other boys had completed their assigned chores. Sokdae was playing ball with them in the yard. It was another of those soccer games where Sokdae's team had fewer players but always managed to win.

As soon as I said I had come to have my clean-up chores inspected, Sokdae, who happened to be on the ball at the time, kicked it to one of his teammates and responded readily. His attitude was that of a conscientious representative of the teacher. As he ran his eyes over the windows I had cleaned, I awaited the outcome with a pounding heart. Even to me, my windows seemed incomparably cleaner and brighter than the windows beside them. If he was in good humor and treated me kindly, I, for my part, would make an effort to get into his good graces with a respectful response, thus casually letting him see my change of heart.

Sokdae examined the windows for a while.

"It won't do, there are stains there still. Clean them again," he said, and then he ran back out to the playground. I felt as if all my blood was rushing to my face. I wanted to make some sort of protest, but before I knew it, Sokdae was on the far side of the playground.

I repressed my feelings with difficulty and examined the two windows again. Several panes on the left-hand side actually seemed to show faint marks where water had run. I figured it was lucky I hadn't made a protest to his face, and I bent to the task of cleaning the stains. As I worked, I noticed other marks and stains, and it was only after a considerable interval of time that I was able to go to Sokdae for another inspection.

At this stage, not only the children in the classroom, but also those in charge of tidying up the class projects had all finished and the soccer match was in full swing. Thirteen on one side, eleven on the other; the teams were made up of the faster boys, and they were using a real leather soccer ball—origin unknown. Not wanting to break up the spirited contest, I waited for some time. Then when I saw Sokdae had scored a goal, I approached him and told him I had come for his inspection.

This time, too, Sokdae promptly left the game. However, the result was the same.

"That's fly shit there, isn't it? Clean them again and clean the dust in this corner."

This time I couldn't take it. I protested half-heartedly. I told him to compare my windows with those done by the boy beside me, but Sokdae cut me off coldly without even looking at the windows I was indicating.

"He's he, you're you. Anyway, I can't pass these windows."

His tone of voice seemed to say I was a special species that demanded rigorous inspection.

In view of this I could do nothing. I climbed up on the sill again and examined every corner of the thirty-two panes. This time I wasn't looking for praise. I directed all my energy to avoid being failed.

The third time Sokdae picked on something else and turned me down again. I smiled a smile I didn't feel, to try and get his goodwill, but it was to no avail. He just said I'd failed, and then he took off to a nearby stream taking the others with him. They had been running and tumbling all this time in the sunshine. It was still hot even though it was early autumn.

I got up on the windowsill for the fourth time and attacked the glass again. But my energy was all gone; I didn't want to move a finger. I sank down on the sill, watching vacantly, like someone in a daze, as Sokdae and the others disappeared into the pine grove at the back gate. Now that I knew success and failure were not related to my efforts, but to how Sokdae felt, I no longer wanted to labor in vain.

Already the sun was setting, and signs of life in the schoolyard were scarce. There wasn't a single child in sight, and the silence was punctuated every now and then by the footsteps, strangely loud, of one of the teachers going home. Several times I felt the urge to throw it all up and run back to my house. I had already relinquished all ideas of resistance, but this was too severe a tyranny to just grin and bear. However, when I thought of being called out by the teacher and of the beating I would get the next day in front of the others after the teacher heard Sokdae's story, and when I imagined Sokdae's gloating face, the urge disappeared on the spot. Instead, although it may have been a bit sneaky, I thought of a better strategy, not at all boy-like, and began to hope Sokdae would be even later. If he wanted to see me suffering, I'd show myself in pain to him, shed a few crocodile tears. Maybe that would alleviate his vengefulness.

The shadow of the huge Himalayan cedar at the western end of the schoolyard had already fully crossed the playground when Sokdae and the others again appeared at the back gate. What happened then is difficult to explain. As soon as I saw them noisily enter the playground, hair glistening wet—they must have bathed—the tears suddenly, and without any effort, gushed from my eyes. The strategy of a moment ago was now completely forgotten: These were real tears welling up from the depths of my heart.

You may feel that all of this was a bit sudden, but analyzed dispassionately now, I think those tears make sense. The only thing pain can wring from a soul that has abandoned resistance and from a mind that has lost its hate is sorrow. I cried then for sadness over my surrender and I cried because my loneliness made me sad.

"Hey, Han Pyongt'ae!"

My sudden tears now changed to uncontrollable sobs. As I clung to the window, I heard someone nearby call my name. I wiped away my tears and looked in the direction of the sound. Sokdae, leaving the others at some distance, had come over alone beneath the window and was looking up at me. His face seemed generous and merciful as never before.

"You can go now. I pass the windows."

From the direction of that face, foggy and indistinct through the well of my tears, came the sound of that gentle voice again. I guess he had divined the exact nature of my tears. Having made certain of an irreversible victory, he had released me from that lonely, tedious fight. All I could feel was an overwhelming gratitude for his generosity. Next day I showed my gratitude by giving him a fountain pen I had particularly treasured.

Although the end of the fight had been all too hollow and my submission all too simple, nonetheless the fruit of submission was sweet—perhaps all the sweeter because my opposition had been long and stubborn. And now that Sokdae was certain I had submitted to his rule, his favors fell like a waterfall.

The first thing Sokdae did was straighten out my fight ranking. A few of the boys who, under his protection, had usurped my ranking unjustly were now made to pay a heavy price; they had to let their ranking go. Sokdae suddenly began to discount the strength of boys who, since my fall in rank, had regarded me as someone of no consequence, and if he heard them call me *sekki* this or *sekki* that, he treated them with utter disdain.

"Yah, do you really think you can beat Pyongt'ae? Can you beat him in a fight?"

Then casually he would suggest, "Pyongt'ae, how about fighting again? Are you going to let a *sekki* like that walk on you?"

Strengthened by this, we'd have the fight—fair this time—in a ring he had prepared. The smoldering resentment I had been feeling gave an extra sting to my fists and brought me easy victory every time. Some boys, frightened by my intensity, raised their hands without fighting. As a result, with just a few fights, I was able to raise my ranking several places higher than it had originally been. I now ranked about twelfth.

I rediscovered friends and games. Once it became known that I had been pardoned by Sokdae, the others no longer tried to avoid me. In fact, noticing that Sokdae had a special regard for me, they tried to get me for their team when we played games.

Infractions of rules, great and small, which had made me a well-known troublemaker, not only in the class but throughout the school, were no longer used against me. My accusers, who used to make such a big deal out of silly things, vanished, and gradually I came to be regarded as a model student. The number of regulations to be observed hadn't suddenly been reduced and I hadn't changed, but the teacher welcomed me warmly as a father would a prodigal son.

My schoolwork gradually returned to normal. Halfway through the second term, I was in the first ten, and in the winter end-of-term exam I got second. And with grades back to normal, the worries of my father and mother, which had been quite severe, disappeared. Once again I was their bright, loving, eldest son.

When you thought of it, all of these things had actually been taken from me by Sokdae. To put it simply, I had just recovered what was mine, and the most you could say of Sokdae was he had given a bit of extra interest. However, now that I had bent to his will, everything seemed like an enormous favor.

The other side of it was that Sokdae's demands were less than I had thought. He didn't seem to deal with me in the same way he dealt with the others; he never asked for anything from me, much less took anything. If I wanted, of my own accord, to give him something tasty or some valuable school item, he didn't want to accept it; and if he did accept it, he always returned the favor several times over. Actually, I remember it was more usual for me to get things from him, though it bothered me that they were all things he had collected from the others.

Also, Sokdae put no burden on me, and he didn't pressure me into doing anything. Sometimes the boys seemed distressed by an unfair burden or pressure imposed by Sokdae, but I never experienced this. As a result, these passive privileges—exemption from burdens and duties—often impressed me more than was really warranted.

All Sokdae wanted from me was to adapt to his order and not to try to destroy the kingdom he had established. This was what submission meant. If you consider this in combination with the basic premise that his order and kingdom were not just, then submission may have been the greatest price I could possibly pay. However, now that I had abandoned my belief in the principle of freedom and any memory of the necessity of reason, submission didn't really feel like a great price at all.

At any rate, in the end—when I had become perfectly inured to his order, a comfortable noncritical resident of his kingdom—there was one more price I had to pay for the favor he dispensed. This involved my skill in painting. In art class I had to do two paintings while the others did one. The second was for Sokdae, who wasn't good at painting. Accordingly, the "Our Skills" display always had two of my paintings hanging side by side, one with Sokdae's name and one with mine. But there mustn't have been much duress because I can't remember clearly whether Sokdae wanted this or whether I made the offer. My guess is that as a subject, residing peacefully in his kingdom, I made the offer spontaneously in lieu of tax or labor service.

OUR CLASS REVOLUTION, SO DIFFERENT from revolutions in the glorious pages of history, came suddenly and in a rather unexpected way. The next year, two months after our teacher had been changed, Sokdae's kingdom, which had seemed so rock solid, was smashed to pieces, almost in the space of half a day, and the iron-fisted ruler, reduced to a mere criminal, disappeared from our world.

However, before telling the story of the immediate origin and course of that revolution, there is something I must first confess. You see, long before that I had been made aware of Sokdae's terrible secret, a secret that in the end shook his kingdom to its foundations.

It was around the middle of December that year, as I remember, that I first learned the truth. It was the end-of-term exam, and in the interest of fairness, the seating arrangements had been mixed up, with the result that Pak Wonha, a good student, had ended up sitting next to me. He was particularly clever at arithmetic and was among Sokdae's ten closest friends. I was always worried about my own lack of ability in arithmetic; this boy's presence beside me gave me, for some reason, a feeling of security.

However, when time was almost up at the end of the two-hour exam, I saw Pak Wonha do something strange. Stumped by one of the practical problems on the exam, I stole a glance across, not with any idea of cheating, but rather because I was curious whether he had written an answer or not. He had already completed his answer sheet and was rubbing out his own name with an eraser. I was suddenly suspicious. You might erase an answer and write it again, but no one ever spelled his own name wrong and had to erase it.

I forgot there wasn't much time left and watched Pak Wonha intently. He kept stealing glances at the supervisor, who was the teacher from another class. Suddenly he wrote a name in the spot he had just rubbed clean, and to my utter surprise the name was Sokdae's. As soon as he had written the name, he looked quietly around. He flinched when his eyes met mine. However, a smile lit up his eyes immediately; he didn't seem to be either warning me or to be in any way afraid of me.

"What were you doing there?" I asked softly, as soon as the break began. Wonha smiled weakly and said, "This time . . . it was my turn for arithmetic."

"Arithmetic was your turn? Does someone else do the other subjects?" I asked again. Pak Wonha looked all around for a moment and spoke in a low voice.

"Didn't you know? Hwang Yongsu probably did the Korean exam in the last period."

"What? And what happens to you fellows?"

"We get Sokdae's grades. When you do his art assignments for him, you can wait for the right moment and present two pictures, but that won't do for an exam, will it? The only way is to change grades with Sokdae."

That's when I discovered the secret of Om Sokdae's extraordinary grade average. The pictures I, without a second thought actually, drew for him also contributed to his straight-A average.

"All subjects in every exam?" I asked. Pak Wonha, speaking in the low tones of a fellow conspirator, answered all my questions, holding nothing back.

"Not all subjects. He usually prepares two subjects himself. In this exam, nature and social science are his own. But the subjects are changed for each exam and the boys who sign for him are changed too."

"And what does Sokdae score in the other subjects?"

"About eighty, give or take."

"That means a drop for you of fifteen marks or more on this arithmetic exam, doesn't it?"

"It can't be helped. All the others do it, too. And Sokdae changes turns fairly, so the loss is evenly distributed. With the exception of Sokdae, our ranking is all according to ability. That's if some lucky boy like you doesn't get in in front of us."

By "us" Wonha meant the seven or eight to whom Sokdae extended special favor.

"But . . . did Sokdae not tell you yet about this? That's strange . . ." Wonha said, worry suddenly written across his face as he saw me standing there more than a little shocked by this secret.

Then, as if to put his mind at rest, he added, "Ah, what about it? It doesn't matter if I tell you now. I mean, you've been doing Sokdae's pictures for him. That's the same as doing a practical art exam for him. And for all you know, you may have to change exam papers with him soon . . ."

But by this stage I was no longer myself. I was already swept up by a powerful temptation.

Armed with this secret, irrefutable proof of misconduct that no one could condone, I was now tempted to reverse the fight just ended. No matter how cold and indifferent the teacher was, he couldn't ignore this sort of misconduct on Sokdae's part. If I was able to catch Sokdae, it would not only be sweet revenge on the teacher who had always supported him, but it would be sweet revenge on my father and mother who hadn't believed me and who had given me such a tongue-lashing. I would become a new hero to the children who, though they grinned and bore it, were certainly suffering. My heart beat quickly when I thought of the return of freedom and reason that I had been forced to abandon.

But when the bell announcing the beginning of

class rang and I saw the face of our teacher, who had come in to supervise the next exam, my heart, which had been in a state of keen excitement, began to sink. Things drag drearily on; new things, changes, are just a bother and a pain. All this was written across his face, recalling to my mind the ignominious failure of the cigarette lighter incident. It seemed that nothing short of irrefutable evidence put in front of his nose would break down that wall of insensitivity and indifference.

I looked around at the others again. They could supply the irrefutable proof, but there seemed little guarantee that they would join me and reveal Sokdae's misconduct to the teacher when they had connived and cooperated with it until now. In addition, to a great extent they were Sokdae's accomplices; hadn't they conspired with Sokdae to obstruct fair grading by the teacher? Thinking of this, I lost even more confidence. Clearly Sokdae had taken the lighter. But when the teacher asked, Pyongjo said he had lent it to Sokdae. And when I provided the boys with a rare opportunity to denounce Sokdae freely, they had turned against me instead.

The sweet fruits of my submission, which I had been sampling now for almost two months—plus some sly calculating—held me back at the time. Actually, apart from damaging my spiritual vanity, being below Sokdae in his order brought me no disadvantages at all. As I've said before, my long, stubborn resistance became a sort of war decoration that brought me various privileges. In some ways I had more freedom here than in the Seoul system, where I was under the control of the student council. Among my classmates, I had as much influence, if not more, as I did as head of my section in Seoul. If Sokdae continued to trip up the others, it would only be to my benefit. Provided I didn't try to be first, I could at least be second without too much effort.

However, the decisive factor that prevented me from running to the teacher was Sokdae himself. Caught between the temptation to turn him in and the temptation to submit, I still hadn't made up my mind by the time exams were all over. I was waiting for final assembly, tormented by my dilemma, when Sokdae suddenly appeared in front of my desk.

"Yah, Han Pyongt'ae," he said. "The exams are all over today. How about going somewhere for a bit of fun?"

I was up on my feet in a flash.

"Where?" I asked. "It's cold outside."

"How about Mip'o? I know a place there where we can have some fun and the cold won't be a problem."

Mip'o referred to the riverbank beyond the pine grove some five *li* from school. To grown-ups it was a bleak place, with just a few factory buildings left over from Japanese times that had been half demolished in an air raid, but for boys it was a fine place to play.

"All right."

"Let's all go," the boys listening beside us said boisterously, even more excited than I was.

I had no good reason to refuse. To avoid appearing suspicious, I went along with the others. This effectively blocked me from seeing the teacher on my own after final assembly. Although I *set out* without much heart for it, I will always remember how much fun I had that afternoon. Almost the entire class wanted to come, but Sokdae chose just ten of us. You might think at first glance that he chose us indiscriminately, but clearly he had his own reasons.

As soon as we arrived at Mip'o and found a spot in the sun in one of the demolished factory buildings, Sokdae turned to the others and asked, "You have money, don't you?"

Five or six boys emptied their pockets and we collected 370 *hwan*, a substantial sum of money to us at the time. Sokdae selected two boys and sent them to buy candy and soda. Then he turned back to the others.

"Which of you live in that village across the water?"

Five or six responded this time too.

"Go home and get some peanuts and sweet potatoes. If you say you're on a field trip with the monitor and the entire class, your folks will gladly give them to you."

After sending this group off, Sokdae finally turned to the rest and said, "Collect some wood. It's warm now, but it'll get chilly, and we have to roast the sweet potatoes and the peanuts."

Now that I had seemingly established myself

within Sokdae's order, I figured that I was included in this final group. But as I was about to go off to gather wood with the others, Sokdae stopped me.

"Han Pyongt'ae, stay here, I want you to help me with something."

This took me by surprise, but it seemed to be motivated by goodwill. Sokdae moved a few stones to prepare a place for the fire, and spent the rest of the time just talking with me. There seemed to be more to it than just excusing me from various errands. I was of course below Sokdae, but now I ranked higher than the others.

When all the boys finally returned, we proceeded to turn the demolished factory building into the greatest playground in the world. Peanuts and sweet potatoes for roasting were placed on the fire, and while we waited for them to roast, we had more candy and soda than we could consume.

We ate, drank, laughed, and played boisterously until the sun went down. We played tag and had a singing contest. Then we had a musical presentation of "Que Sera Sera" that made us keel over with laughter. One boy dropped his trousers and took out his little unripe pepper; he pulled out the foreskin as far as it would go, and using this as the strings and his index finger as the bow, he mimed playing the violin. Another boy twisted his hands marvelously into a trumpet and made a very good imitation of its sound, while yet another stuck out his pot belly and beat it *tat–tat–tat* like a drum. Beside them was a boy imitating a singer and another circling the area doing a series of handstands and somersaults.

But the extraordinary thing was Sokdae's attitude; he was twice as friendly as before. He treated me as if I ranked differently than the others, and he directed the entertainment of the day almost as if it were a banquet for me. Actually, you could say that for that day he had raised my ranking to the level of his own. Perhaps this is too much of a leap. It was clear, however, that Sokdae, feeling some threatening sign from me, was trying to win me over with the taste of power.

Needless to say, I was completely intoxicated by the special sweetness Sokdae had allowed me to taste. As I returned home in the fading light, I erased from my mind any idea of telling the teacher Sokdae's awful secret. I hoped and believed that his order, his kingdom, and the special benefits I enjoyed, would last forever. And yet, before four months had passed, these hopes and beliefs had collapsed.

Now, as promised, I will tell the immediate origin and course of that singular revolution that resulted in Sokdae's downfall.

Having moved up to sixth grade, we began in earnest to prepare for the middle-school entrance examination. We also had a new teacher.

The man who was put in charge of our class was very young, just a few years out of teachers' training college. Although he didn't have much experience, his ability and hard work were recognized, and he was specially chosen to take charge of our entrance-exam class.

Indeed, from the very first day, our new teacher showed he was different from his predecessor. And from the very first day, he noticed something strange about our class. He rebuked us implicitly in our very first general assembly.

"Why is this class so lifeless? Like fools always watching to see how the next boy is reacting?"

Within three days of taking over the class, his unusual perceptivity was closing in on the essence of the problem. We had a new class monitor election that day because we were now in sixth grade, and when Sokdae was elected with fifty-nine of sixty-one votes, the teacher flew into a rage.

"What sort of election is this? Unanimous except for one invalid vote and his own vote? We'll have the election again."

Sokdae, seeing his mistake, immediately tried to take charge of the situation. When he got fifty-one votes in the next election, the teacher's reaction was the same.

"What's this? The other nine, apart from Om Sokdae, are all one vote each? What in heaven's name is the point of an election where there is no one to compete with?"

Venting his anger like this, he glared in turn at Om Sokdae and at the rest of us. Given the results of the election, he had no choice but to recognize Sokdae as monitor. Still, you could say that this was the beginning of our singular revolution.

"Fools! So full of silly fears! Eyes straight ahead! What sort of behavior is this for boys? Looking to see what the next boy is doing!"

Every time there was a difficult math problem, he called Sokdae and made him solve it. Sokdae seemed to sense the crisis. He tried hard to defend himself, but the teacher seemed far from satisfied. On the day after the first evaluation exam, he asked Sokdae, "How can you be so good in exams and so bad in class? I don't understand you."

Although he wasn't fully aware of the existence of Sokdae's deception, there was always a suspicious look in his eyes. Nevertheless, he gave a grudging recognition to Sokdae's established authority and to the existing order that regulated our class.

The teacher's suspicious attitude had considerable influence on the class. It gradually became clear that he wasn't on Sokdae's side, and that far from trusting Sokdae unconditionally like our former teacher, he actually mistrusted him. The boys, who wouldn't budge last year despite everything I did, now began to wriggle of their own accord. Even though they didn't dare challenge Sokdae to his face, there were little acts of opposition. It became not uncommon for boys to go straight to the teacher rather than to Sokdae to solve a problem or dispute.

I'll say it again and again—Sokdae was something special. Even if he was older than us, he was still no more than a boy of fifteen or sixteen, but he knew when he had to have forbearance and when he had to give ground. He seemed to have an instinctive feeling for this balancing act. Things he would have handled formerly with his fists, he now handled instead with a little frown; things that once incurred a frown, he now met with a gentle smile. He stuck it out grimly. Boys quick on the uptake were now careless with their "tribute," but he held back from punishing them. And he absolutely never said, "Lend me that" or "That's lovely."

I think that Sokdae was well aware of the danger of substituting exam papers. But this was one thing he couldn't stop doing. It was like being on the back of a tiger. All he could do was race on to the end. I suppose he could have given up his almost perfect grades, but to abandon the title of "first in the school," which he had held now for two years, was too big a price.

Things finally came to a head when the exam scores were announced after the first regular exam of the year at the end of March. That day the teacher came in with a black, stone-cold face and immediately read out our scores. Then he said, "Om Sokdae with an average ninety-eight marks, first in the entire grade, the rest of you all outside the first ten in the grade. This is a puzzle I'm going to solve today."

As soon as he had finished, he called Sokdae sternly.

Struggling to look calm, Sokdae went up in front of the teacher's desk.

"Brace yourself against the corner of the dais and stretch out your legs!" the teacher commanded without any further explanation. When Sokdae had stretched out, the teacher lifted a thick stick, which he had carried into class along with his roll book, and brought it down hard on Sokdae's backside.

Suddenly the room, hushed as if splashed with cold water, was filled with the sound of the beating and of Sokdae's harsh breathing as he tried to endure the pain. It was the first severe beating I had ever seen. The stick, thick as a baby's wrist, soon split at the end and bits of it began to fly off. But what shocked me more than the beating itself was the very fact that *Sokdae* was being beaten.

Sokdae getting a beating! So pitiful, so helpless—it was a shock not just to me, but to all the boys in the class. And it was obvious that this sort of reaction was precisely what the teacher wanted. The stick in the teacher's hand had been reduced to half its size, but still the beating continued. Squirming his body in an effort to bear the pain, Sokdae finally collapsed to the floor with an awful groan.

The teacher seemed to have been waiting for this moment. He left the fallen Sokdae, went to the desk, found his exam paper, and returned to Sokdae's side. Sokdae was once again arched over the floor.

"Look at this, Om Sokdae, do you see the mark of the eraser where your name is written?"

That was when I realized the teacher had discovered Sokdae's secret. Suddenly, rather than feeling sympathy or fear for Sokdae, I began to be more curious about how it would all turn out. I wondered what would happen if Sokdae denied any misdeed as he had done in the case of the lighter, and if the boys would unite in support of him as they had done then.

"I am sorry."

This was the disappointing response eventually elicited. After all, he was just a boy of fifteen or sixteen, a human being with a body that surrenders easily. Perhaps the teacher had administered the harsh beating peremptorily to elicit precisely this response.

When the others heard Sokdae's words, there was another invisible shock wave. Sokdae is giving in! It was astonishing to see this happening in front of their eyes. I felt this way too. I flinched involuntarily when I heard him apologize.

As soon as the teacher had received Sokdae's admission, he went on immediately to the next phase, without giving Sokdae much chance to think.

"Fine," he said. "Get up on the desk, kneel down, back on your heels, and hold your hands up!" He approached Sokdae as if he might start beating him again at any moment. In view of what happened afterwards, Sokdae must still have been in shock from the surprise onslaught. He got up on the desk, waddling awkwardly, like a wild animal driven by a whip, raised both hands, and knelt down.

Seeing Sokdae like this had a strange distorting effect on how I perceived him and the teacher. The old Sokdae seemed much the same height and build as the teacher; in fact, if anything, Sokdae seemed bigger. But on that day, the kneeling figure of Sokdae on the teacher's desk had suddenly grown small. Our monitor of yesterday, big and healthy, had vanished without a trace, and in his place was just an ordinary boy like the rest of us, getting an unseemly beating. In comparison, the teacher seemed to have grown suddenly to twice the height and build. And he was standing there looking down on us like some omniscient giant. I wouldn't have been surprised if all the boys had the same feeling. For all I know the teacher may have had this in mind from the beginning.

"Pak Wonha, Hwang Yongsu, Lee Chigyu, Kim Munse . . ."

The teacher called out the names of six boys. They were the best students in the class, the ones who had taken turns doing Sokdae's exams for him. With white faces they inched timidly toward the teacher's desk. The teacher's voice was now a little softer.

"I am aware that throughout the exams last month you boys took turns erasing your own names and writing another name. So, how about it? Will it take a beating to get you to talk? Or will you answer straight if I ask nicely? Who was it? With whom did you change grades?"

The teacher hadn't quite finished his questions when Sokdae's eyes, which had been half-closed and unfocused until now, were suddenly raised and gave out a frightening light. His shoulders, which had been drooping from the weight of his uplifted arms, were now straight and stiff. The boys flinched when they saw this. But the tide had already turned. The boys had seen Sokdae's weakness, so they chose without hesitation to side with the strong teacher.

"Om Sokdae!" the boys cried in unison, and immediately Sokdae closed his eyes as if he were in pain. Although Sokdae's lips clearly were closed tight, I swear I heard a moan coming from somewhere deep inside.

"Good. Well now, how did you come to do such a thing? We'll begin with Hwang Yongsu."

The teacher spoke in a slightly more gentle,

coaxing voice. With the stick lowered as he spoke, he seemed to be saying he might forgive them if they gave him a straight answer. Pinning their hopes on this, the boys, almost as if Sokdae wasn't even there, began to give their reasons. Things like "I was afraid he'd hit me," or "he used to punish us for no reason," or "I didn't want to be left out of our games"—the sort of things I had experienced myself.

"All right. And how did you feel during all this?" the teacher asked.

Again, the boys let everything out. Half said they were wrong and felt guilty, half said they were scared the teacher would find out. But what I couldn't fathom at all was the teacher's reaction. As soon as the last boy had finished, his face twisted sternly.

"Is that a fact?" he spat, as if in ridicule. Then glaring coldly at the six, he shouted in a voice loud enough to make us all flinch. "All of you, brace yourselves against the dais and stretch out your legs!"

Then he began to administer the beatings, ten whacks for each boy. The beatings were so harsh that each of the boys collapsed to the floor two or three times. When it was over, the classroom was filled with the sound of their sniveling.

"On your feet, all of you!"

When the sniveling finally died down, the teacher got the six boys on their feet and spoke to them, barely holding back the anger in his voice.

"I wouldn't have laid a hand on you if I hadn't thought it was absolutely necessary. I could have excused the switching of the exam papers because you were pressured by Sokdae. But when I heard how you felt all this time, I just couldn't take it. What was rightfully yours was taken from you and you weren't even angry. You bent to unjust power and you weren't ashamed. And the best students in the class, too. If you continue to live like that, the pain you will bear in the future will be so great, the beating I gave you today won't even compare. It's horrible to even imagine the kind of world you'll create when you become grown-ups. Now kneel down on the dais, back on your heels, hands up, and think about what I've said."

Perhaps the teacher was trying to teach us something that was just too difficult. No one among us there understood what he really meant; indeed, thirty years later, some of us still don't.

When the teacher finally turned back to the rest of us sitting in our places, the six boys, their faces a mess with tears, were already kneeling side by side on the dais.

"All we have discovered so far is that Sokdae and these boys switched papers. But that's not enough. If we are to remake our class, we have to start with a clean slate. I am inclined to think that Sokdae is guilty of a lot more. Now I want you all in turn, beginning with number one, to tell us everything Sokdae did, or anything you've suffered at Sokdae's hands."

He began softly this time, too. But the edge came back in his voice when he saw everyone flinch and hesitate under Sokdae's glare.

"I heard what happened last year from your fifth-grade teacher. He said no one wrote down any of Sokdae's misdeeds, so he figured there was no problem in the class and continued to put his trust in Sokdae. It's the same for me today. If you don't tell me about Sokdae's other misdeeds, I have no choice, now that punishment for the exam-paper-switching incident is over, but to entrust everything once again, just as it has been, to Sokdae. Is that what you want? Talk! Beginning with number one."

This had an immediate effect. Actually the boys were not as wishy-washy as I had thought. They just didn't know how to combine their power. The burning anger and humiliation they felt in their hearts was no different than what I had felt when I challenged Sokdae. And the anticipation of reform—reform that had seemed so close and was now being threatened—gave them the courage to hang on and fight.

"I lent Sokdae my pencil sharpener and he didn't give it back. He took a steel marble from me one week when marbles weren't restricted."

When number one talked, number two, three, and four began to talk too. Tales of Sokdae's misdeeds went on and on like water spilling from a dam. There were sexual things like making them lift the girls' skirts, or forcing them to soap their hands and masturbate; and there was economic exploitation, too, like making the children of shopkeepers contribute so much money every week, the children of farmers bring fruit and grain, and the children of peddlers bring hardware items to exchange for taffy. Then there were things like charging a boy 100 *hwan* to appoint him as a section head, or collecting expenses to buy necessary items for a clean-up-the-environment project and keeping part of the money for himself. And most of the story also came out of how for one whole term the previous year he had made my life a living hell.

One extraordinary thing was the attitude of the boys making the denunciations. At first they could only look at the teacher as they revealed their stories haltingly, but as one followed the next, their voices gradually grew louder, their eyes began to glitter, and they began to glare right at Sokdae at they spoke. Finally, they began to confront Sokdae directly rather than just denouncing him to the teacher, and they laced what they said with language they wouldn't have dared to use before.

Finally my turn came, number thirty-nine.

"I really don't know anything," I said, looking straight at the teacher; instantly the classroom became quiet. But a moment later it was my classmates not the teacher who were raging at me.

"You really don't know?"

"*Sekki!*"

"Don't you have any guts?"

The boys began to abuse me as if they would jump on me if the teacher wasn't there. Somehow despite the force of their attack, I stood my ground.

"I really don't know. I only just transferred in."

Looking straight ahead at the teacher, I repeated what I had said. The others began to berate me even more roughly. The teacher turned to calm them down.

"I see," he said. "Next, number forty!"

My reason for saying I didn't really know about Sokdae's misdeeds was half sincerity and half pride. Although I had been particularly close to Sokdae over the last three or four months, he had never shared his secrets with me. What I had suffered at his hands that first term had all been indirect. I had no proof. And most of it had already been revealed by the others. In addition, my own position for that year in fifth grade left me at an extraordinary disadvantage in trying to uncover Sokdae's misdeeds, which were hidden in every corner. Because for half the year I was Sokdae's only opponent, and for the other half his right-hand man, I never made the kind of friends to whom I could open up. As a result, you could say that all I had was the vague feeling that things were wrong; I really had no way of knowing for sure what was happening secretly in the classroom.

Yet I suspect the strange impulse to defend Sokdae I felt that day sprang from the attitude of the boys in front of me denouncing him. Those who were most zealous and belligerent in divulging Sokdae's misdeeds could be divided roughly into two groups. One group was made up of boys who had earnestly desired Sokdae's favor, but who, right to the end, for one reason or another, had failed to get it. The second group was comprised of those who until that very morning had been at Sokdae's side and who had been his accomplices in numerous misdeeds. Although it doesn't necessarily take a long time for a man to repent—a butcher, they say, can become a Buddha if he lays down the knife—I just wasn't convinced by their sudden display of righteousness. To this day, I have a hard time accepting people who suddenly convert from one religion to another, or people who suddenly change their ideology, especially when they rant and rave in front of others. To tell the truth, if I wanted to attack Sokdae, I didn't really lack ammunition, but presumably I kept silent that day from a certain pride that was a reaction against these boys. They seemed to me no more than traitors who had waited for Sokdae to fall before jumping on him and walking all over him.

Number sixty-two was the last. When he finished his denunciation, the bell rang for the end of the first class period. But the teacher ignored it.

"Good, I consider it fortunate that you have rediscovered your courage. Maybe we can entrust the future to you after all. However, you have to pay a price, too—first, the price of your former cowardice, and second, the price of the lesson it provides for your future lives. It's not easy to find something again that has been lost. If you don't learn now, the next time something like this happens, you'll just wait for a teacher like me. No matter how painful or difficult the situation, you won't get up and find what you've lost for yourselves; you'll always wait for someone to find it for you."

When the teacher had finished, he went to the

broom closet and took out a mop with an oak handle. He stood in front of the dais once again and ordered in a low voice, "From number one, come out in turn, one at a time."

Each of us got five slaps that day. We got a harsh beating, just like the boys who had gone before, and once again the classroom became a sea of tears.

"Well now, your teacher has done everything he can for you. Go back to your places, all of you. Om Sokdae, too. I want you to discuss among yourselves how you can make this the best class anywhere. You've learned already how to run a meeting, and you know about the decision-making process and about voting. From here on in, I'll just sit down and watch," the teacher said, looking very tired after the beating. He went and sat in the teacher's chair in the corner of the classroom. Just looking at him as he took out his handkerchief and wiped the sweat from his forehead, you could tell the severity of the beating we had just received.

I thought the boys here didn't know, or had forgotten, how to run the class council. Now that they had the opportunity, this wasn't so at all. They were a bit awkward at first, but in their own way they knew how to get things done as well as Seoul children. Their faltering for words was short-lived. Soon they recovered their confidence; they made motions, seconded, endorsed, and voted. They decided first to form an interim management committee, which would supervise an election to select the officers who would form the new council committee.

So there you have it. You may ask why I called Sokdae's downfall revolutionary, since there wasn't anything very revolutionary about it. But although we were indebted to our teacher for the strength and will to destroy Sokdae's old order, the building of the new order was the product of our own strength and will. I have to give our teacher credit for encouraging us to remember what had happened and to make sense of it on our own.

Kim Munse, class vice-monitor, was chosen by a show of hands as interim chairman, and he proposed that, without the complications of an election, we choose an interim committee to supervise and record the vote. Instead of having five separate elections, he suggested we pick one digit and entrust the task to the members of the class whose number ended in this digit. The boys agreed to this, and, by a show of hands, the six students whose class number ended with the digit five were decided on as interim committee members.

Finally, the election took place; it lasted for two hours. Formerly, only monitor, vice-monitor, and treasurer were chosen by election, but this time, the five heads of various subsections of the council and even the class section leaders were chosen this way. This was the start of an "election for everything" trend that went on for some time, bringing much confusion to our class.

The counting of votes for monitor was almost complete. There had been no nominations for the election, with the result that the names of nearly half the class were written on the board.

Suddenly there was the sound of the back door of the classroom being thrown open. All eyes had been glued to the election figures on the blackboard. Looking around, we saw Sokdae on his way out the door. He stopped and glared fiercely at us. "Do what you like, *sekkis*!" he cried.

Then he ran out into the corridor and escaped. The teacher, busy keeping an eye on what we were doing, had lost track of Om Sokdae for a moment. He called Sokdae's name and rushed out after him, but he wasn't able to catch him.

The boys recoiled for a moment at this sudden development, but the counting of votes began again and soon there was a result: Kim Munse 16, Pak Wonha 13, Hwang Yongsu 11, one boy each with 5, 4, and 3, five or six boys with one vote, and two invalid votes, making a grand total of sixty-one votes.

Sokdae didn't get a single vote. Presumably Sokdae had run off because he couldn't bear to wait for the humiliation of the count becoming official. However, he wasn't just running off from that humiliating moment; from then on, he never came back to school or to us.

Although it is embarrassing, allow me to explain what was behind the two invalid votes. One of them was undoubtedly Sokdae's vote, and the other was mine. My vote wasn't a reaction against the revolution. It wasn't prompted by any wish to cling to Sokdae's collapsed order, nor was it a question of nostalgia for lost power. From the fire lit by the teacher, the ardor of revolution was already spreading inside me, and my expectations for the new class we would build equaled the expectations of the others.

However, in the actual moment of choosing a leader to direct the class, I found myself suddenly confused. All the boys who were superior to the rest in study, fighting, or other skills, were guilty of many of the same offenses as Sokdae. The best boys had either helped Sokdae steal the teacher's trust and favor by taking exams for him, or they had been Sokdae's accomplices, enabling his unjust order to prevail. They were the ones who had given me the hardest time when I stood alone in my difficult opposition to Sokdae; and in the sudden reversal whereby I became closest of all to Sokdae, they were the ones most envious.

At the same time, I couldn't bring myself to endorse blockheads who, although they were sixth-graders, couldn't recite their multiplication tables, nor could I vote for boys who began to cry before a fight even began and were despised even by the runts in the front of the class. And I couldn't vote for myself—I mean, until that very morning, I had been content with the special favor Sokdae bestowed on me. So, my vote, in conscience, was really an abstention disguised as an invalid vote. Not being able to feel optimistic about the reform, from that day on I developed a wretched nihilism which has stuck with me ever since.

Nevertheless, the elections that day all proceeded smoothly, and we were so thorough in our insistence on self-determination that section leaders were elected by the members of their sections exclusively. Much of the order that regulated our lives was modified. Everything was decided by debate and vote—it put my Seoul days to shame. As a result, all forms of compulsion that didn't come from school or teacher were abolished. Korea's April 19 Revolution occurred shortly after Sokdae withdrew, but I wouldn't dare suggest it had any influence on young people like us.

Of course we experienced the confusion and the exhaustion that comes with revolution. And for several months afterwards, we paid an exorbitant price, within and without, for not having been able to achieve the beginning or end of that revolution ourselves.

The greatest cause of confusion and exhaustion

within the classroom was our own fragmented consciousness. Encouraged by the teacher and driven by the unbounded exhilaration of victory, one group pushed itself forward too forcibly, while other boys, not fully awakened from the repression of Sokdae's order, fell far behind and could only push forward inch by inch. The boys on the council were just the same. Some of them, devoted to the noble cause of democracy, constantly changed their minds, reflecting the wishes of the confused majority; others, unable to transcend Sokdae's authoritarian tradition, quietly dreamed of little Sokdaes. In addition, there was the new suggestion box, which didn't serve its proper function as a citizen's complaint forum, but rather worked as a source for plots and allegations, so that once a week a council member was changed.

Outside school, what bothered us most was Sokdae's revenge, which was indescribably audacious and cruel. Every day, for nearly a month after Sokdae left, one corner of the classroom was empty. Sokdae would block some vantage point to school, and the boys in that area would not be able to get through. The injury the boys suffered was far greater than a day's absence from school. He would drag them off to some secluded place and for half the day exact the price of betrayal. And if he didn't go that far, he cut their bags with a sharp knife or threw the boys, books and lunchbox included, into a sewage pit. The revenge was so persistent and tenacious that eventually the boys openly regretted throwing Sokdae out.

However, as time went by, the challenges within and without were gradually met.

First to be dealt with was Sokdae. The teacher's method of solving the problem was rather unusual. For some reason, the teacher dealt with boys who were absent because of Sokdae with beatings and scoldings that were harsher than ever, even though the matter was really beyond their control.

"Four of you dragged off for the entire day by one boy? Fools!" he would cry. Or, "Were both your hands tied? Clowns!" he would shout, and then he beat them mercilessly. We didn't understand why he did this, but the effect was soon apparent. Eventually, five particularly tough boys from the cattle market clashed with Sokdae. Sokdae was more ferocious than ever, but the boys jumped on him as if their lives depended on it, and in the end Sokdae got his butt out of there, not being able to take on all five of them. The teacher made a point of giving the five boys great face in front of the rest of us, by presenting each of them, to all of our envy, with a copy of President Kennedy's *Profiles in Courage*, which was very popular at the time. The next day, the same thing happened with the boys from Mich'ang. Afterwards Sokdae never appeared again.

In comparison, the teacher's attitude to our confusion within was quite different. No matter how noisy the classroom, or how confused we grew over our classwork as a result of misunderstanding or divided opinion, the teacher ignored it completely. When council meetings dragged on for three or four hours on Saturday afternoons, or when the monitor and vice-monitor were replaced once a month in some new disturbance caused by secret information about some paltry offense in the suggestion box, he never gave a word of advice; he just watched quietly.

As a result, almost a whole term went by before the class returned to normal. Once the summer holidays were over, the middle-school entrance exam loomed only three or four months away, which totally occupied the boys' attention. More important, I think, experience had nurtured in us a certain self-control. During those five or six months of squabbling, nitpicking, clashing, and squirming, we had learned what it means to discipline ourselves. However, a lot more time had to go by before we were able to understand what our teacher really thought as he watched over us during all this time.

When class life returned to normal, my twisted consciousness also slowly returned to its former state. To put it in adult terms, my civic awareness, which faltered when I cast that vote of abstention in the election for the new monitor, was soon restored. In the end, my old faith in freedom and reason returned. Still, from time to time—for example, when I saw boys who liked shouting in public going on and on with endless doubts about something absolutely trivial, or when a project required concerted efforts and I saw boys not participate for various reasons, with the result that our class fell behind other classes—I would remember the convenience and efficiency of Sokdae's rule. The temptation to return to it was greater now that it was forbidden, but it remained no more than a temptation.

AFTER THE FIGHT WITH THE MICH'ANG boys, Sokdae disappeared, not just from among us but from the town. I heard sometime later he had gone to live with his mother in Seoul. Having lost her husband early, she had left young Sokdae with his grandparents and remarried.

Afterwards my own life became hectic. Harassed by the demands of school and parents, I don't know how I got through the rest of the term, but my frantic study for the entrance exam paid off, and I just managed (barely) to get into a decent school. The next ten years were spent in competition and exams. Accordingly, the memory of Sokdae, which had remained vivid for some time, gradually grew dim. When I finally ventured out into the world, having with great difficulty gone through a first-rate high school and a first-rate college, the memory had become no more than a meaningless specter, as if Sokdae was a character who had only appeared once during a brief nightmare. However, it wasn't just the hectic pace or difficulty of my own life that made me forget Sokdae. There was nothing in my environment during this time to remind me of that period. Growing up in a world of first-rate schools and model students, I didn't have to experience again that sort of repression or deprivation of values. Ability and effort, in particular mental ability and scholarly inquiry, were the decisive factors now. Passing through these places, where autonomy and reason were the norm, Sokdae remained buried in the back of my mind as an image of injustice.

And so the next time Sokdae began to surface in my consciousness was after army service, when I had been wallowing in the slough of life for some ten years. At first, as behooved the product of a first-rate school, I had joined one of the big conglomerates. Two years later, feeling it was like a castle made of sand, I left and began again, this time in sales. I did not want to waste my youth and talent working for a group where there was no freedom on the job, where the management was full of hypocrites, and where the promotion process was unjust. Dreaming of the salesman's era soon to come, I spent nearly three years zealously selling the products of big conglomerates, faulty products backed by exaggerated advertising. As I ran around with catalogs for medicine, insurance, and car accessories all in the same bag, I ended up missing out on the latter half of the seventies and the last years of my youth. By the time I discovered that a salesman in this country is in one sense just another customer, and in another a disposable product made by one of the big conglomerates with a life expectancy of two years at most, I was already the wretched father of a family and in my mid-thirties.

At this stage I was shocked into taking a look around. The large conglomerates, which I had felt to be castles made of sand, were actually prospering. My old colleagues who had stayed on were being promoted to section heads and to department chiefs, their faces shining with success. One of my school contemporaries had gone into real estate, and already, from leases alone, he was a regular in the golf clubs. A friend of mine opened a hole-in-the-wall agency of some sort, made a pile of money selling some product—he didn't even know what it was for—and now was swaggering around. And another peer who I thought had become a soldier was sitting pretty in an undreamed-of post in the central government. One fellow, who failed even as an entrance exam repeater and finally got into a school that was absolutely the pits, somehow had got himself a Ph.D. in America and was now a highly respected professor.

I was in a hurry. By this stage I had no patience for the process that led to this kind of success, nor the social structure that made it possible, but was solely interested in the fruits my friends and acquaintances were enjoying. In a word, I wanted to squeeze into a corner of their rich table. But my very urgency buried me that much deeper in the slime of my life. I sold my 19 *pyong* apartment, which I had managed to buy only with great difficulty, and I set up an agency in a high-risk business with money pulled from here and there. This splendid venture left me unemployed and living in a 2 *k'an* rented room.

It was then that I took a step back and managed to see the world more clearly. I began to have the feeling that I had transferred into a strange place.

Here my grades in my old school and my other proud achievements were of no use; it was as if I had been thrown into a cruel kingdom that ran things as it wished. Here Om Sokdae began to reappear from the dim past.

In a world like this, Sokdae would certainly have become class monitor again—of this I was sure. Sokdae would decide study ranking and fight ranking, and possessions and pleasures would be dispensed as he willed. From time to time, I dreamed I had happily rediscovered that class and was enjoying life close to Sokdae's side, just as in the old days, and I would wake up disappointed.

Fortunately, the real world was not like our old class, and there were still a few places that could use the knowledge I had acquired in a first-rate college. The place I found was a private academy. Although I had some difficulty adapting to my new life as a lecturer, I was able to make enough of an income to look after my wife and children. And after only a few months, life improved enough for me to dream of having my own home. However, the conclusion I had reached about Sokdae didn't change in the slightest.

Friends I met from time to time from elementary-school days very often supported this conclusion.

"Om Sokdae is really something! I saw him going by, in the backseat of a luxury car; he was sitting back in total comfort."

"I went back home, but the whole trip was ruined by Om Sokdae. I got a few friends together for a drink, but he was all anyone talked about. I don't know what it is he's doing, but he came back with two young men and literally swept the main street with money before he left."

The men spoke with wonder in their voices, but I had the feeling that they were nonetheless belittling him.

Our Sokdae couldn't be that small-time. If this was the best Sokdae could do in terms of vulgar success, how could I explain my life with its thick shadow of failure? And our Sokdae wouldn't have his power and money so readily apparent to the eye. He would "run this class" from some secluded secret place. If I were willing to put aside all belief in freedom and reason, he would call me and invite me to sit by his side. If I gave him the benefit of even part of my ability, he would give me almost anything.

Finally, I met him too. It was last summer. I had just managed to get a few days off on account of the university entrance exam and I was bringing my wife and children to Kangnung. Because I meant this to be a real vacation, I had no intention of skimping on spending. But at the station, I found that all tickets for the express train were sold out, and the train we were forced to travel on was indescribably bad. We each had a child on our knee because the children were still so young they didn't warrant their own tickets. The children were loud, the corridors full of passengers, and the air conditioner didn't function properly. As soon as we reached Kangnung, we got off the train and headed for the exit. Suddenly, I heard a familiar voice cry out behind me.

"Let go. Let go, can't you?"

I turned and saw that the cry came from a sturdy young man, whose arms were held by what appeared to be two detectives in plainclothes; he was struggling to break loose. He was dressed in a beige suit and he wore a matching brown tie; his left sleeve had been torn in the altercation. The face behind the sunglasses seemed strangely familiar. I stopped without realizing it.

"Jump all you want. You're caught like a flea. The station is completely covered," one of the detectives spat coldly, taking a shiny pair of handcuffs from his belt. The prisoner struggled all the more when he saw this.

"*Sekki!* Haven't you come to your senses yet?" This came from one of the detectives.

The other detective, unable to take any more, struck the prisoner across the mouth. The impact sent his sunglasses flying. The prisoner's face was now revealed. I was shocked to see it was Om Sokdae. Thirty years had gone by, but I could recognize at a glance the high blade of the nose, the strong chin, and the flashing eyes.

I clamped my eyes shut as if I had seen something I shouldn't. A vision from twenty-six years ago arose before my eyes: Sokdae kneeling on the dais with his hands raised. But he had none of the tragic beauty of a fallen hero nor anything else special about him; he was just one among the poor ineffectual lot of us.

"What's wrong, love?" my wife asked worriedly, pulling my sleeve gently. She was standing beside me, not knowing what was going on. I opened my eyes and looked again in Sokdae's direction. Sokdae was being dragged away, wiping his bloody mouth with his cuffed hands. He glanced at me as he passed, but he didn't seem to recognize me at all.

That night, beside my sleeping wife and children, I drank until it was late. In the end, I shed a few tears, but whether they were for me or for him, whether from relief for the world, or from a new pessimism, I still really don't know.

# About the Author

YI MUNYOL IS ONE OF SOUTH KOREA'S foremost contemporary novelists. Born in 1948, his early years were unhappy. His father's defection to the North in 1951 during the Korean War put enormous pressure on the young family, burdening them not only with poverty and prejudice but also with the psychological pressures that come from constant police surveillance. Yi Munyol had a checkered school career, plagued by financial and other problems. After mandatory army service, he worked as a reporter and teacher before making a name for himself with such works as *Son of Man* (1979), *Winter That Year* (1980), *The Bird with Golden Wings* (1982), and *Hail to the Emperor* (1983). A musical, *The Last Empress*, was based on his short story "The Fox." Adapted for the stage by Yi

Munyol, it played at venues including New York's Lincoln Center.

Yi Munyol's writing has been translated into eight languages, and he has won most of Korea's prestigious literary awards, including the Donga-ilbo Award for Aspiring Young Writers, the Writers Today Award, and Dongin Award.

*Our Twisted Hero* (1987), winner of the Yi sang Award, was written when the nation was still raw from the Kwangju Massacre and writhing under the stranglehold of dictatorship. It was made into a major motion picture in Korea. Subsequently, Yi Munyol wrote *The Poet* (1992), ostensibly a fictional account of the life of Kim Sakkat, a Choson dynasty wandering poet, but in effect a thinly veiled account of his own life and the vicissitudes endured by his family. He followed this with a popular series of Chinese romantic epics in translation. His most recent work is *Song of Songs* (2000).

CPSIA information can be obtained at www.ICGtesting.com
Printed in the USA
LVOW07*0202070616

491492LV00007B/29/P